"I can see you're dressed in scrubs, but I can't just let you crack open this man's chest without confirming your identity."

Glittering sapphire eyes met hers and her breath locked in her throat. He was even more stunning in the flesh than he was on screen...almost impossibly so. She was aware the team around them was continuing with the CPR—compressions were being quickly but steadily counted aloud, monitor alarms still rang out, reminding them the patient's vital signs were critically outside of parameters. She knew what was going on around her, but for a moment, the center of her focus was the two deep blue eyes looking back at her, laser-like, penetrating, silently assessing. Her determined resolve not to find him attractive wavered. Straightening the front of her uniform, her instinct telling her to look away, she held his gaze.

"Max Templeton," he replied, one dark eyebrow raised and clearly having completed his appraisal of her, "cardiothoracic consultant." Was he trying to suppress a grin?

Dear Reader,

I'm completely thrilled to share Max and Lois's story with you and really hope you enjoy their romance. Delving into each of their backstories has been emotional, as has discovering how they coped with and worked through their challenges both individually and, ultimately, together to find their happy-ever-after.

Look out for my next story, where mysterious A&E consultant Dexter Stevens is forced to choose between opening his firmly locked heart or losing the only woman he's ever loved, cancer survivor and full-of-life nurse Tilly Clover.

Happy reading!

Colette x

NURSE'S TWIN BABY SURPRISE

COLETTE COOPER

MEDICAL ROMANCE

Harlequin®
MEDICAL ROMANCE

Recycling programs for this product may not exist in your area.

ISBN-13: 978-1-335-94279-1

Nurse's Twin Baby Surprise

Harlequin Enterprises ULC
22 Adelaide St. West, 41st Floor
Toronto, Ontario M5H 4E3, Canada
www.Harlequin.com

Printed in U.S.A.

To my biggest cheerleaders, my lovely family.

CHAPTER ONE

THE ANTICIPATION OF meeting the new consultant was undoubtedly the cause of Lois Newington's butterflies and the excited, almost tangible buzz in the air. He'd arrived two days ago, when she'd been away on a course, so she hadn't yet met him, but he seemed to be the subject of every conversation between the staff. She was ready for him, though. Ready and determined not to fall at his feet as it seemed most of the rest of the hospital staff had done. TV's Dr Sex-on-a-Stethoscope might well look like a movie star, but Lois was off men... totally.

The cool and not unwelcome swish of air around her bare legs as the cubicle curtain was pulled back told her that they had company. Otherwise ignoring the newcomer, she instinctively took a step forward to allow them into the cubicle behind her. She wasn't going to allow whoever it was to distract her even for one second from the emergency she was dealing with.

It was probably a junior doctor. Junior staff often wanted to watch a cardiac arrest to gain experience—well, they could watch, as long as they didn't get in the way.

The clear, confident instructions she called out were completely by the book—a CPR masterclass. She'd done this a thousand times, and even though the understandable adrenaline surge made her heart bang against her ribs, she controlled its rate with accustomed resolve, kept herself two steps ahead of the rest of the team and appeared as cool as the proverbial cucumber. If there was one thing scumbag Emilio couldn't have criticised her over, it was the fact that she was good at her job.

'Airway secure?'

'Secure and air entry all areas, Sister.'

Lois glanced at the cardiac monitor. 'VF. Shockable rhythm. Charge, please.'

The shrill tones of defibrillator rang out as it fuelled itself with electrical charge, but the doctor's gaze wasn't focussed on the patient—it was fixed on the newcomer who was standing silently, right behind her. The back of her neck prickled.

She looked around the cubicle. Senior nurse, Tom, on chest compressions, was counting aloud, but everyone else was looking past her right shoulder, and they all seemed to be standing a little bit taller and a little bit straighter than they had been before the stranger's arrival.

Her stomach lurched. She didn't need a sixth sense to know instantly who they were looking at. The newcomer was Max Templeton, surgeon to the stars and Emilio the scumbag's much anticipated replacement. She didn't turn around. The defibrillator's beep signalled that it was ready.

'Stand clear.'

Everyone moved away from the bedside.

'Shock, please.'

A dull thud of electricity shot, bullet-like, into

the arrested patient, causing his body to arch in response.

'Checking rhythm…'

She held her breath, silently praying that the erratic ECG trace on the monitor would settle to a normal sinus rhythm. If it didn't, this patient's chance of survival would plummet.

'VF.'

The commanding male voice from just behind her, almost made her jump.

'Shock again…now.'

'Charge,' called Lois.

What was he doing? He couldn't just turn up and take over.

A junior doctor took the command and depressed the charging button. The defibrillator whined as the electrical charge built within it.

'Stand clear,' she called.

'Shock.'

Max Templeton's command rang out loud and clear, the command on her own lips silenced by his. She didn't have time to turn around and explain that *she* was leading the arrest and had been for the last five minutes. Didn't he know the protocol? He must do. He was just making his presence felt—just like Emilio, and just as she'd expected he would.

Emilio had gone, leaving her to try to put her life back together, but his replacement was going to be exactly like him—she just knew it. The only difference was that she wasn't going to fall ridiculously head over heels for Max Templeton—not in a million years.

The dull thud of the electric shock entered the patient and Lois turned her attention to the monitor as the spikes on the ECG settled.

Damn, he was still in…

'VF. Shock again.' The male voice behind her cut in with an air of authority no one could ignore. 'Get me some wire cutters and a thoracotomy set. I may need to reopen his chest. He's had adrenaline, I assume?'

He moved from behind her and stood at her side, almost but not quite touching her arm with his. Still she didn't look at him, but there was no doubt who it was standing beside her, ignoring protocol, taking command, flooding the air between them with crackling anticipation.

So here he was at last, the much anticipated, famous and infamous Max Templeton. His reputation as a brilliant surgeon wasn't in doubt, and she was keen to see him in action. But what she knew she *wasn't* going to appreciate was his reputation as a man who thought he was God's gift to medicine…and women. By the time Emilio's six-month contract had been drawing to a close, and he'd been preparing to go back to Italy—back to his wife and the toddler daughter that he'd somehow neglected to tell her about—she'd have welcomed whoever replaced him. Anyone was better than the deceitful, lying cheat she had the misfortune to call her ex. But he was being replaced with another smooth operator… TV heartthrob Max Templeton.

She wasn't going to give him the satisfaction of turning around to look at him; much as she wanted to.

'Dr Harper—charge, please.' The junior doctor depressed the button. She had his attention back.

She swept a glance around the bed. 'Stand clear…'

'Shock.'

Max Templeton's clear command came only a split moment before hers. She swung round to face him as she heard the shock being delivered. He was overriding her. Did he think she was incompetent? Or was he just being the arrogant egomaniac she'd expected he would be?

'Was that a yes or a no to the adrenaline?'

His tone was composed but firm. Two deep blue hypnotic eyes burned into her, requiring an answer—eyes she'd seen hundreds of times on screen, in newspapers and in magazines. Eyes whose true power could only be felt when face to face with them.

'Begin chest compressions.'

She tore her gaze away from him to instruct the team. She had exactly two minutes to reply to him whilst the next cycle of CPR continued. Turning fully towards him, she let her gaze travel upwards over his tall frame, and the further up his body her eyes rose, the harder her heart banged in her chest.

He was a finely tuned athlete, with an impressive, strong-looking physique, sun-kissed skin, broad shoulders and well-defined pecs not hidden by the navy scrubs he wore. He looked like a glossy ad for designer aftershave. Only the scrubs and the stethoscope draped casually around his neck made him look like a doctor and not an Olympian.

She swallowed. It *was* him.

Don't look at him with 'starstruck' written across your face like everyone else is.

Somehow, she found her voice. Professional Lois kicked in and she briefed him on the situation with the patient.

'Yes, as protocol. The patient suddenly dropped his BP to sixty over thirty, central pressure was down at two, heart rate one ten, and then he went into VF. He's had two cycles of CPR and that was the third shock of the second cycle. And you are...?'

Impossibly, her heart rate notched up further still. *Had she really said that?*

There was little doubt as to who he was, but he shouldn't just rock up and expect everyone to know him. He wasn't wearing any ID and, a stickler for correct protocol, Lois felt a need to point it out to him right there and then that was almost overwhelming.

She turned back to the team. 'That's two minutes. Check rhythm again, please.' She'd timed her reply perfectly.

The team paused to let the chaotic green lines on the monitor settle, but the high-pitched, continuous beep told anyone who wasn't staring at it that it had settled into an ominous flat line.

'Asystole.' *Damn.* 'Continue CPR.'

'We need to do a thoracotomy.'

Again, his tone was calm, but his words made Lois draw in a breath. He wanted to perform open heart surgery on the intensive care unit? It was unheard of.

But Max Templeton had taken a sterile pack from the shelf and stepped forward, claiming his space, and all eyes were fixed on him. Ripping the pack open, he dropped it onto the bed and spread the sterile field flat to reveal the array of silver surgical instruments within it.

'Continue CPR until I'm gloved up and ready,' he ordered.

The team did as they were instructed, swiftly swinging into action, restarting the methodical, well-practised processes which they hoped would prolong this man's life long enough for Max Templeton to remedy the underlying cause.

Despite the fact that he hadn't introduced himself, and wasn't wearing his ID, everyone knew it *was* him, of course. He was one of the best-known faces on the planet. But he'd just assumed everyone would know who he was and that just reeked of arrogance. No one else had questioned him, but charlatans had been known to masquerade as medical staff in hospitals, often by being brazen. And this man certainly had more than a touch of the brazen about him. He shouldn't just stride in here and expect that everyone knew him…but that had been exactly what he'd done.

Well, she wasn't having it. She spoke quietly but directly.

'I can see you're dressed in scrubs, but I can't just let you crack open this man's chest without confirming your identity.'

Glittering sapphire eyes met hers and her breath locked in her throat. He was even more stunning in the flesh than he was on screen...almost impossibly so. She was aware the team around them were continuing with CPR—compressions were being quickly but steadily counted aloud, and monitor alarms still rang out, reminding them the patient's vital signs were critically outside of normal parameters.

She knew what was going on around her, but for a moment the centre of her focus was the two deep blue eyes looking back at her, laser-like, penetrating, silently assessing. Her determined resolve not to find him attractive wavered. Straightening the front of her uniform, her instinct telling her to look away, she held his gaze.

'Max Templeton, cardiothoracic consultant,' he replied, one dark eyebrow raised, clearly having completed his appraisal of her.

Was he trying to suppress a grin?

But it was gone before she could decide, and then, much to her astonishment, he took her by the shoulders and gently but firmly moved her to one side before snapping on the sterile gloves.

'I operated on Mr Ferns yesterday and replaced his aortic valve in order to keep him alive. I'm not about to let him die today.' He picked up the wire cutters. 'Dressing.'

Everyone had been right—he was something

else. Most surgeons wouldn't attempt this procedure outside of a theatre.

She watched him like a hawk as she too quickly drew on a pair of sterile gloves. If he was going to attempt this they had to move fast.

Reaching out in front of him, she tore the dressing off the patient's chest. 'This is pretty irregular, Mr Templeton.'

'He has a cardiac tamponade,' he replied, slicing through the chest sutures with ease. He glanced at the three junior doctors opposite him across the bed. 'One of you needs to glove up to hold a retractor.' He addressed Lois again as he began to cut through the wires holding the patient's sternum together. 'He'll die if I don't drain the blood from the pericardium.' He snapped through a wire. 'And I'm not about to let that happen.'

Clearly.

But she wasn't going to be silenced that easily. 'You can't do a thoracotomy on the unit.'

'Watch me.'

'You could attempt pericardiocentesis.'

'I know.' He cut through another wire with a snap.

'It's less traumatic.'

'I know.' He snapped through the last wire and eased the sternum apart, placing a retractor inside the cavity and handing the end of it to one of the juniors, instructing him to pull gently but firmly.

'But you're not going to.'

His swift glance and raised eyebrow gave her his answer.

Lois threaded her arm through his. The jolt as her skin met his was as unwelcome as it was shocking. She pressed thick piles of swabs against the edges of the wound, stemming the bleeding, applying pressure. The oozing red liquid soaked through the gauze, warming her gloved fingers. She had no qualms about calling for help if Max Templeton didn't pass muster, but up to now she was satisfied with all his actions.

All his actions, that was, except the way he looked at her and made her insides quiver. *That* was completely unsatisfactory.

'Tamponade. Pass me a—'

Lois placed a large syringe and long needle firmly into his outstretched palm. The faint look of surprise in his eyes was just a tad satisfying. She hadn't been an intensive care and theatre sister for four years without knowing how to assist with a thoracotomy.

'Thank you, Sister…?'

'Newington.' She pointed to her name badge whilst holding out a tray ready for the syringe, her forearm brushing his and sending a spark into her which could rival the jolt from the defibrillator.

Why did these cubicles have to be so damn small?

The staff had all been correct in their assessment of this new consultant. He was undeniably gorgeous and, much to her surprise and annoyance, she'd been ridiculously conscious of her heart hammering in her chest since the moment their eyes had locked minutes before.

She didn't want this.

Emilio had slunk back to his family in Italy, leaving her self-esteem battered and bruised, six months ago. The last thing she needed was to fall for the charms of another schmoozer. Well, she wasn't going to.

Get a grip, Lois. This man lives in a different world—he's surrounded by glamour. He isn't even going to notice your existence beyond what you can do for his patients. And if you didn't know that before Emilio slimed into your life, you certainly do now.

Max Templeton's reputation went before him. Since leaving medical school he'd quickly made a name for himself as one of the world's leading heart surgeons, and soon celebrity patients had been queuing up to be treated by him. His film star good looks and charismatic charm had made him the perfect TV doctor, and he seemed to spend as much time on the red carpet as he did operating. He'd recently returned to his roots in the NHS to pioneer an antenatal cardiac screening programme, but he'd only signed a four-month contract for some reason.

The only other thing she knew about him was that his reputation for mending hearts rivalled his well-known reputation for breaking them. And after the recent dark chapter in her life that had been Emilio, she wasn't going anywhere near his replacement, clearly cut from the same cloth. No one was ever going to crush her like that again.

'Fifty mils aspirated.' He was utterly focussed

and completely in control. 'He's very bradycardic—there's not enough pressure.'

Reaching back into the chest, he began internal cardiac massage, rhythmically squeezing and releasing the heart, attempting to bring it back to life.

Lois watched the green lines on the monitor. They were either flat or barely moving. The numbers were flashing, telling them what they already knew—that they were into desperate measures territory, and the patient's life was balanced on the thin knife-edge between life and death.

Shifting her gaze, she watched as Max, calm but still intensely focussed, his jaw set, tiny beads of sweat appearing on his forehead, continued to demand that life return to his patient. He appeared to be true to his word—he really didn't want this patient to die.

No one dared to breathe. Only the rhythmic hissing and clicking from the ventilator and the long, continuous flat beep from the monitor filled the silence. All eyes were on Max Templeton, his gloved hand inside his patient's open chest. Time stood still.

Was this much-esteemed surgeon as good as he was cracked up to be?

'Suction.'

It wasn't a question or a request. Already poised with the suction tube in her hand, Lois inserted it into the pool of ruby blood which had collected in the chest cavity, clearing it so that Max could see.

'Better pressure on the arterial line,' she advised,

glancing at the monitor at the side of the bed, break-ing the silence, taking charge, in control as always.

She might not be svelte, slender and beautiful—*thanks, Emilio, for confirming that*—but this was something she was good at. At least no one could argue with that.

'Over sixty,' agreed Max. 'Enough to perfuse his brain. But the acid test is what happens when I take my hand off the heart. Ready?'

It was intoned as a question, and no one in the cubicle was going to say they weren't. He stilled his hand and focus moved to the cardiac monitor where, if the intervention had worked, the waver-ing, erratic green lines would show signs that life was returning.

'Sixty-five.' Lois willed the screen to give her the figures she wanted. 'Pressure's seventy.'

Suddenly there was hope.

'Good.' He withdrew his hand from the open tho-rax, wiping his brow with his forearm. The tight-ness in his face, jaw and neck slipped away as he let out a slow breath. 'How do we know the patient isn't still bleeding and won't tamponade again?'

The three junior doctors looked back at him—deer in headlights.

And that was when his whole demeanour changed.

'Any ideas, guys? No problem if you don't—this is a great learning opportunity.' He gave a wry grin. 'Not that the patient would see it that way.'

Taking the retractor from the junior doctor, he placed it back into the sterile tray before resting his fingers on his patient's wrist. He studied his audience as if awaiting a response, his famous smile completely changing his face.

The act was so sudden and the effect so startling that Lois was forced to make sure her mouth wasn't gaping open.

How could someone go from Mr Cool and Arrogant to Mr Relaxed and Happy in a second?

'The answer, is that we don't,' said Max. 'We have no way of knowing if the pericardium will fill up again. If it does, and any of you are on duty, you can call me—day or night, whether I'm on call or not. Okay, thanks everyone. Show's over, let's get back to work.'

Had the Max Templeton who'd first walked in and so rudely taken over suddenly been replaced with another Max Templeton, who knew what politeness was and even had a sense of humour?

Suddenly, her perception of him as irretrievably arrogant as hell had a severe dose of doubt thrown over it. She let out a breath. It sure as hell was going to be interesting working with this man—she'd never seen anyone like him.

So what was it that made her feel so uneasy?

His star status? His super-confidence? His apparent lack of respect for protocol? His willingness to push the boundaries to save a patient?

Or was it the fact that when he'd locked his eyes on hers he'd made her heart skip a beat or ten?

The junior doctors filed out, the very attractive female of the three smiling at Max as she drew the curtain behind her in an unnecessarily coy way, making Lois roll her eyes in disbelief. She was so glad she wasn't one of those fawning females who were so obvious it was embarrassing.

'Do you want an echocardiogram?' she asked.

Why was she suddenly so annoyed? What did she care if staff flirted with him?

As long as it wasn't done in an unprofessional way or in an inappropriate situation.

But the reason her question to Max had come out so abruptly was as obvious as it was annoying—the junior doctor was slim and pretty, and had enough self-confidence to allow her to flirt openly with someone and even maybe to think that the other person might welcome it.

Lois had never been able to flirt. Whenever she'd tried it, she'd felt silly. It was probably a skill you learnt as a teen—going out with friends…at the school dance. And she'd never done any of those things, had she? As her mother's carer, she'd never been able to indulge in those rites of passage. She'd never been round to friends' houses, excitedly getting ready for a night out, talking about boys, experimenting with make-up, trying each other's clothes on. Flirting was untrodden territory for her.

She hadn't even flirted with Emilio. Lord knew how they'd ended up getting together. He'd done all the running, though, hadn't he? And she'd been stupid enough to fall for what had turned out to be empty compliments.

'No,' Max replied now. 'The tamponade has been drained, and the figures are good. Shall we suture him up?'

Tom slipped out of the cubicle, returning a moment later with a suture pack, which he placed on the bed before turning to Lois.

'Okay if I carry on now?' he asked.

Lois opened her mouth to respond, but once again Max was quicker.

'Sure.' Then, placing his stethoscope in his ears, he bent to listen to his patient's chest.

Tom raised an eyebrow at Lois and grinned at her, mouthing *Told you!* before slipping out of the cubicle, leaving them alone. Lois bit her lip.

'I just thought you'd want a scan to check the valve.'

That was normal procedure, and she was duty-bound to remind him—even if he was one of the most eminent cardiac surgeons in the world.

'There's nothing wrong with my valve, Sister Newington.'

He spoke with uncompromising certainty, reaching for the sterile gloves from the suture set Tom had opened, snapping them on before looking at her directly with his laser blue eyes and flooring her with his completely disarming smile.

'A scan won't be necessary.'

Lois watched him as he began to close the patient's chest, absorbed once more in his work. There was no doubt that his clinical reputation as the best was completely justified. He'd just cracked open this man's chest, and that was pretty rare outside of an operating theatre setting. He'd saved a patient's life and he looked as if he wasn't even trying.

He'd made an impressive first impression...on

COLETTE COOPER   23

the whole. But he blithely ignored protocol, wasn't wearing any ID, and spoke to the staff as though *he* ran the unit instead of her.

What everyone had told her seemed to be correct—Max Templeton was something else, and she knew she was gaping at him in exactly the same starstruck way everyone else had been. Well, she wasn't about to allow another consultant to stroll into her unit, rinse and repeat...

'You seem a little irked about the lack of ID badge, Sister.'

His voice broke into her thoughts sharply. She straightened up but he wasn't looking at her. He was working intently on his patient, dark head bent, long fingers moving to and fro with swift expertise as he sutured. He was mesmerising...in more ways than one. But his professional expertise was all she wanted to be mesmerised by—she wasn't interested in anything else.

'ID should be worn at all times,' she managed, a little surprised that she could speak. Suddenly, after what he'd just pulled off, her issue with him not wearing his ID seemed trivial.

But was he trying to make a point?

'I was about to start a theatre list when I got the arrest call and I hadn't quite finished getting dressed.'

He turned to face her, the intensity of his blue eyes making her breath catch in her throat and her thoughts spin so she couldn't find the words she needed to speak.

What was he doing to her?

Whatever it was it was completely unwelcome. She was off men...period.

He turned back to the patient and she took a moment to breathe again.

'And if I can't trust my ability to place an aortic valve correctly...well, it's time to give up, frankly.'

Lois knew full well that she was staring at him with very poorly disguised incredulity. Humility wasn't one of his strong points, then.

But then he smiled, and his blue eyes twinkled, lighting up with shining stars of mirth.

'I know what you're thinking, Sister Newington.'

That you're astoundingly gorgeous?

'I doubt it, Mr Templeton.'

He lowered his gaze, focussing once more on his patient. 'You think I'm an arrogant ass.'

Lois couldn't help it that her mouth fell open. He was right, though—that was what she'd been thinking. As well as thinking that she wanted to spend for ever gazing into his eyes. Which was such a contradiction she couldn't quite believe she was thinking it.

Don't do this, Lois—get your sensible head on again.

'Wearing ID is mandatory for all staff, whether you're a cleaner or a surgeon, and I'd be grateful if you could remember that the next time you step into my department—there's good reason for it.'

There...sensible Lois was back in the room.

Snipping the end of the last suture, he tossed the needle and forceps into the opened thoracotomy pack and checked his watch, apparently ignoring her comment.

'Finished?'

She wasn't usually one for stating the obvious, but the quizzical look in his piercing eyes told her she'd probably done just that. She swallowed, managing to hold his gaze even though she desperately needed to look away. Max Templeton had people falling at his feet all the time. Well, she wasn't going to be one of them.

'All yours, Sister Newington.' He swept an upturned palm towards the patient.

Focus, Lois.

Stepping forward, she leant in to clean the wound. But Max didn't stand aside, and her arm brushed his once more, sending a bolt of electricity through her.

Why didn't he move?

His nearness was warming her—way too much.

'I can take care of everything now.'

Please leave.

She needed to breathe normally again.

'I'm sure you can, Sister. Please, carry on—I'm just monitoring his heart rate a moment longer.'

Trying to pretend he wasn't there, she tore the backing from a dressing and placed it over the suture line, smoothing it down carefully, her mind whirling, weighing him up, trying to process what had happened over the last hour, wishing he hadn't made her knees suddenly struggle to take her weight.

Was he good at what he did?

Undoubtedly.

Did she think she could work with him?

Of course she could—she'd managed it before, hadn't she? Working with surgeons who thought they were the best thing since sliced bread was an all too familiar challenge. She'd ridden the storm that was Emilio Bartello and survived—just.

Did she like him?

Not so easy to answer. How could she like someone who had his reputation with women? Men like him thought they could do whatever they liked, with whoever they liked. And if she'd learned anything in the last year...if her relationship with Emilio had taught her anything...it was not to trust men. Especially good-looking, successful men.

But for the last hour her heart had been hammering in her chest as if it was trying to break out—and that hadn't been solely due to the clinical situation they'd found themselves in.

CHAPTER TWO

HE'D LIED—he didn't need to look at the monitor. The rhythmic beeping told him everything he wanted to know about the condition of his patient's heart. But it had been a close call, and dealing with close calls brought out both the best and the worst in him.

On the one hand, it focussed him so acutely that he was able to give the patient everything he had, calling to mind everything he'd ever learned and giving that patient the very best chance they had of survival—the very thing he wished he'd been able to do all those years ago, when his own brother's life had been in his hands and he'd failed him.

On the other hand, it turned him into what others might interpret as an arrogant ass. He knew he had work to do on that score, and although he tried to control his reactions to being in life-threatening emergencies, and not to come across as over-confident and condescending, he knew he didn't always achieve it.

He'd have loved to be able to rock up to an emergency and feel nothing—churn out the correct interventions with a cheery smile and an easy manner, make everyone think he was cool, calm and a ray of sunshine as he made life-and-death decisions. But life-threatening emergencies churned up memories from long ago that he'd spent his life desperately trying to keep buried, and when he was suddenly confronted with them he feared becoming the twelve-year-old boy who'd failed his twin.

The day William had died—the day that had destroyed everything—he'd made a promise. He wouldn't ever let the same thing happen again. Becoming a heart surgeon had made good on part of that promise—doing everything in his power never to lose a patient—and what he'd come here to St Martin's to do now would complete it.

Sister Newington currently thought him an arrogant ass—he'd seen it in her eyes. He wasn't. He just couldn't lose a patient. This patient had been lucky; his condition was stable. Which meant he could turn his attention fully to the ICU sister who'd clearly got the wrong impression of him and did not feel the need to hide it.

Looking at her was now both possible to do and impossible not to. He'd been briefed about her by the hospital's CEO when she'd been trying to persuade him to come here to St Martin's. Not that he'd needed persuading—he had his own reasons for coming. It was to fulfil a long-held promise from many years ago—a way to make up for what had happened to William…possibly. Learning that the sister at the helm of the intensive care unit was a consummate professional who ran the place like a well-oiled machine was simply a bonus.

No one had warned him, however, that Sister Newington had seductive come-to-bed eyes, curves to die for and a seriously kick-ass attitude which had shot a dose of undeniable lust through him. He knew his ranking in the world of cardiothoracic surgery was as a world-leading heart surgeon, but somehow she'd just turned him into a first year again, questioning his decision to open the patient's chest and berating him for not wearing his ID.

She was right, of course, to question him. But no one had questioned him over anything in a long while. It was oddly alluring…

'Well done, by the way.' He lifted his eyebrows, mildly surprised at the words which had left his lips.

'For not kicking you out and sending you to get your ID?'

She began to gather up all the strewn empty packages from the bed and bundle them into a disposal bag.

'Not in the best interests of the patient at that particular point.'

She lifted her eyes and met his gaze, holding it as time stood still.

And then she smiled.

And his stomach tightened.

Her green eyes were exquisite. No one had warned him about those either.

'I meant for dealing with me performing open heart surgery in the middle of your unit. I got the feeling you weren't keen.'

She clearly hadn't been, but it had been the only option and she'd dealt with it like the consummate professional she'd been described as—much to his admiration and relief.

'Just don't make a habit out of it.' She glanced at

the post-arrest untidiness of the cubicle with an exaggerated theatrical sigh. 'It makes a hell of a mess.'

Her eyes sparkled and suppressing his own smile became impossible.

'Apologies, Sister; let me help.'

He picked up the used wire cutters, fully expecting her to tell him to get back to Theatre and do his list. Most nurses didn't allow consultants to clear up.

'Very good of you.' She threw a pair of artery forceps into the receiver he was holding. 'Many hands make light work and all that.'

Lois Newington was evidently not most nurses. And he didn't want to look away.

Stop it—that's not why you're here.

He picked up one of the discarded retractors. She certainly lived up to her reputation—confident, competent, in control… The perfect combination for her role as Sister on the ICU.

'Well, your intention was good, but so far you've picked up the sum total of three items.'

She nodded towards his hands and he looked down at them. He had indeed contributed very little to the clearing up operation.

'Not used to it, I assume?' she said.

He looked at her, confused. 'To what?'

'To clearing up.' She rolled her eyes and took the receiver dish from his hand. 'Typical. You might as well get back to Theatre, then.'

And he was a first year again.

'Yes, I've got a bypass to do.'

What was she doing to him? He was a consul-

tant surgeon—the best in the land—and he was being told off.

The odd thing was…he didn't mind—in fact, he was rather enjoying it.

What?

'I know.'

She turned, reaching up for the curtain to pull it open. His errant gaze wandered down her body and his breathing deepened as her uniform rose to reveal the backs of her bare knees.

'Mr Swain. He's coming here post-op. He'll be in bed three. I promised him I'd be here.'

'Right…'

His difficulty in processing the thoughts suddenly flooding his mind took him by surprise, and somehow, unnervingly, he couldn't suppress them. But Sister Lois Newington wore that blue uniform like he'd never seen anyone else wear it…

Stop.

He'd come back for one reason only—and it didn't include getting involved with anyone. His reason for becoming a heart surgeon had been no random choice. Neither had the fact that he'd given so much of his time, energy and own money to St Martin's either. Getting this project over the line wouldn't bring William back, but it would help to prevent any more families from being torn apart. And that required giving it everything he had. Because he'd promised his twin that what had happened to him wasn't going to happen to anyone else—not if he had anything to do with it.

'I'll see you after, then,' he said now. 'If you're still on duty.'

Was he asking her? Did he want to know?

The shocking answer to both questions was yes.

'Well, that depends on how long you take with Mr Swain.'

She pulled the curtain back to reveal the rest of the unit going about its daily business as usual—ventilators clicking, monitor alarms pinging—and suddenly he remembered where he was. He needed to be in Theatre. Yet here he was, being drawn to this sassy, captivating woman, hoping she'd still be on shift later when he came to check on his patients.

'I'll be here.' She turned back to face him. 'I never leave the department until all the patients are settled in post-op—I'd never sleep.'

Inexplicably and confusingly, his shoulders relaxed at the thought. He wasn't surprised at her answer. He could well imagine that she wouldn't sleep unless she knew the patients under her care were as stable as they could be and were being well looked after. She looked completely earnest, and again the surprise that he found it was utterly natural to smile at her shocked him.

It was because he valued dedication.

It wasn't for any other reason.

He wasn't interested in engaging in anything personal. He enjoyed the company of women—of course he did—and there were always plenty of women who were happy to spend the odd night or so with him...mostly because of who he was and his connections in the TV business. But longer term? No, thanks. Long term meant allowing someone else into your head, and his head was a mess no one needed or would want to get to know.

Their eyes met once more, kicking his pulse into overdrive as the ever-present lively hum of the busyness of the unit faded into the background, leaving just the two of them, locked in a long moment, rooted to the spot, standing alone amongst the hustle and bustle.

Suddenly she lowered her gaze and turned away, hiding that gorgeous smile, digging her hands into her pockets, glancing around the unit, her sassy confidence gone.

What had changed?

He had to go, but wanted to stay.

Keep it professional, Templeton.

Professional and superficial. He didn't want to get involved with anyone, even briefly. There was too much else to do. The promise he'd made to William over twenty years ago was about to come to fruition.

Remaining in London for all those years when all he'd wanted to do was run away had been hell at times, but necessary, and he'd promised himself that if he achieved his goal he'd leave London for a new job in California—finally get away from the city he'd grown up in…the city where his life had changed for ever and his young world had come crashing down around him.

Now being able to leave London was so close, and he wanted to do it as quickly as possible and get the hell out of there.

'I should get back to Theatre,' he said.

'Yes.' Glancing at her fob watch, she took a pen from her breast pocket and began busying herself jotting obs down on the huge chart at the end of the bed. 'The sooner you get started on Mr Swain, the sooner we can get him settled in and comfortable here.'

And just like that, sassy Lois was back in the room.

'Thank you again for your help.'

With a reluctance he didn't want to admit to, he walked away, feeling compelled to look back and struggling not to. Pushing open the swing doors leading into theatre suite number four, he called out to a passing nurse.

'Call for Mr Swain from Ward Six; I'll be ready in five.'

He strode into the scrub room and stood before the long trough sink, turning the taps on with his wrists. He smoothed the dark orange iodine solution up his arms, lathering, scrubbing, rinsing, lathering a second time, his mind swimming with unwanted images of Lois that wouldn't go away. Drying his arms roughly he eased them into the sterile gown and shrugged it onto his shoulders.

Lois Newington.

He had to clear her from his head.

Those eyes.

Reaching for sterile gloves, he snapped them on.

Those curves. That sassy, sparkling confidence.

And yet there was vulnerability too—she'd exposed just a flash of it before she'd hidden it by busying herself. What was the cause of it? She intrigued him.

'Ready, Max?'

He looked up sharply. It was Toby, his anaesthetist.

'Patient's asleep—whenever you're ready.'

'Ready.'

Thinking any further about Lois would have to wait. Actually, he really didn't want to think any further about Lois at all, did he? He'd be leaving soon. London had stopped being his home a long time ago and had become just a place he needed to be so that he could fulfil his duty. And as soon as that duty was done he'd leave. He had to...had to get away from the place and the memories it held. Leaving the city was the prize he'd promised he'd award himself for all the years of training, exams and long shifts, all the years of research. The prize for staying even when it was the last place on earth he wanted to be.

That was the plan and nothing would change it.

'That was all very dramatic, wasn't it?' said Tom as he and Lois prepared infusions in the clinical room.

'The thoracotomy?'

She held up a bottle of anaesthetic, piercing the rubber stopper with a needle, watching as tiny bubbles of air rushed through the fluid, allowing it to flow.

'He swept in like a superhero—were his underpants on over his scrubs?' Tom grinned. 'It's the first time you've met him, isn't it?'

'Um-hum…'

Lois held up the giving set, rolling the regulator with her thumb, sending the milky liquid into the tubing. She was trying to forget how Max's intense blue eyes had locked onto hers and made her heart thud heavily in her chest, but it had proved impossible all afternoon. And now even the mention of his name had a similar effect.

'Welcome to the fan club.' Tom wore a dreamy but then suddenly pained look on his face. 'Why are all the handsome men straight?'

He sighed dramatically, making her laugh.

'Don't give up, Tom, your knight in shining armour will come along one day. Come on—let's get these up.'

Nodding towards the infusions, she was glad to end any talk of Max Templeton. His dark, handsome profile as he'd held his patient's heart in his hands and saved his life was etched on her mind, even though she'd spent half the afternoon trying to shake herself free of it. But she wasn't interested in Max Templeton in any other way than for his surgical ability. And she most definitely wasn't interested in romance.

But he'd be back on the unit later…after Theatre.

Her heart rate picked up again. The devastating smile he'd flashed at her when they'd been clearing up had flooded her face with heat and made her turn away from him to hide it. Hopefully he hadn't noticed. Hopefully she would be able to control it the next time she saw him. But Max Templeton was like no other man she'd ever met—and, damn it, her unruly, misbehaving heart flipped once more in her chest.

CHAPTER THREE

BUSYING HERSELF AT the bedspace, Lois ran through the checklist. Oxygen and suction, infusion pumps and paperwork—all ready to receive the patient. The double doors behind her clunked open.

Her heart missed a beat. *Max*. He was early.

The porter grinned as he steered the bed carrying the patient into the space, slotting it between the banks of equipment before locking the brakes.

'Evening, Sister.'

'Evening, Dom.'

No Max Templeton.

Lois returned Dom's smile, but the fluttering butterflies had become stones and they sank to the pit of her stomach as the anticipation of seeing him again dissolved into unmistakable disappointment.

Straightening her uniform, she looked to Toby for handover.

'All went well,' advised the anaesthetist as he disconnected the oxygen from the portable cylinder, handing the tubing over to her. 'On pump triple bypass, as planned. Vein graft from left leg: two units of blood. Norad is on four mils an hour. PCA. Last blood gases were okay. Chest drain in situ and patent. Obs stable. Post-op instructions in the notes.'

'Family?'

Lois transferred the leads from the small portable monitor to the large monitor above the bed, which sprang into life as different coloured lines of varying waveforms appeared on it, showing the patient's vital signs.

'They're all up to date and will visit tomorrow. Templeton's happy with everything. Anything else?'

'No, I think that's everything. Thanks, Toby.' The butterflies in her stomach fluttered into action again, dancing at the mention of his name.

'Well done, Mr Swain.' Toby touched the patient's arm. 'Get a good night's sleep; you'll be well looked after here.'

Trying to control the fluttering, Lois smiled at the anaesthetist. She liked Toby—he was warm, gentle, and he cared about his patients. His was a friendly, comforting face, and he was down to earth and immensely likeable. He'd married her best friend, Natalie, one of the staff nurses who worked on the unit. They were expecting their first baby and were incredibly happy.

It was lovely to see two people so in love.

What must it feel like to be loved by someone so much?

Maybe she'd never know. All her life her mother had told her she wasn't lovable—wasn't attractive enough for anyone ever to love her. After her death, she'd eventually come to realise her mother's cruel words about her weight and plainness had probably been her way of keeping her there in the family home, to look after her. She hadn't wanted her to get ideas above her station and believe she could leave home to be with a lover, or even a husband one day.

And it had worked. In fact, it was still working.

Unpicking the reasons behind those cruel taunts had been a long, difficult process, but Lois had been making some slow, steady progress. Right up until the time Emilio had come along, taken her for a mug, and smashed that progress into the rocks so hard that now there was nothing left of it.

'I'll see you in the morning, Mr Swain.' She touched his hand lightly, having satisfied herself that he was stable. 'Get some sleep now.'

'Thank you, Sister…for keeping your promise.'

She hadn't eaten and it was late. Making her way out of the hospital, she told herself she was looking forward to a quick cheese on toast when she got home. She walked past the chapel and stopped. It would be quiet in there, and empty—a good opportunity for her to practise for the service on Sunday. Supper could wait another half an hour—and anyway, she had enough reserve on her hips to keep her going for a while.

The door to the chapel creaked slightly as she pushed it open. It was dark save for the small collection of flickering prayer candles on a table. The sweet scent of melting beeswax filled the air. Flicking the end light switch, to illuminate the soft lights on the altar, she made her way to the front, slipping off her fleece and placing her bag on top of it on one of the wooden chairs. The light partially lit up the coloured stained-glass window behind the altar and the jewel-coloured panes glowed richly. The chapel was silent save her footsteps on the terracotta tiled aisle, and at this time in the evening it was highly unlikely she'd be disturbed.

Perfect—just how she liked it.

Church choir had been one of her very few escapes when she'd been growing up—one of the few places, apart from school, she'd been allowed to go. It had provided her with some much-needed warmth and friendship over those difficult years as she'd tried to navigate her way through school and college whilst also being her mother's carer.

'Ave Maria' was perfect for her mezzosoprano range. The melody was exquisitely beautiful, delicate and emotional. But the only way Lois had ever been able to sing it aloud in front of other people had been to imagine no one was there—always ensuring she was on the back row of the choir, hiding away behind the others and pretending no one else was there to hear her, see her, judge her.

She'd vowed that if she ever had children, she'd encourage them to sing at the tops of their voices, whenever they liked. But it wasn't something she herself had ever been able to do...unless she was alone.

Imagining the opening notes, she closed her eyes and began to sing—softly at first, but quickly building the volume and intensity as the song progressed, projecting her voice to fill every corner of the chapel, allowing it to escape from her fully, ebbing and swelling with the melody, reaching its crescendo and falling away serenely to its end.

She drew in a deep breath, refilling her lungs with the air she'd given to the last series of notes.

The unmistakable scraping sound of a wooden chair on a wooden floor made Lois freeze. Sud-

denly alert, a shot of adrenaline making her heart
bang uncomfortably in her chest, she squinted to
the back of the room. A dark figure stood up and
began to walk towards her, down the central aisle.
Instinctively, she took a step backwards as the light
from the altar fell on his tall frame, illuminating
him.

Max Templeton.

What was *he* doing here?

He stopped halfway down the aisle, looking
at her sheepishly, his hands in his pockets. She
couldn't move.

'It's only me.'

Only me? Probably the one person in the whole
world she would have chosen not to be there right
then, and he said, *'Only me.'* As if him suddenly
coming out of the shadows like a prowling panther
was nothing.

Could he hear her heart banging like a bat out of
hell against her ribs?

'I can see that…now.'

'Sorry… I didn't want to startle you.'

He began to walk towards her again, and it was
all Lois could do to hold her ground and not step
further backwards. He stopped just before the first
step of the altar, three steps below her, his eyes
level with hers, and the light from the flickering
candles flamed the dark indigo pools, drawing her
into them.

'You have a beautiful voice, Sister Newington.'

Heat flooded through her, flushing her cheeks
with unwanted warmth.

You have beautiful eyes, Mr Templeton.

'Oh… I was just practising…it's better with the music.' She plunged her hands into her pockets.

'It's beautiful without—perfect, in fact.'

His eyes were hypnotic, mesmerising… They seemed sincere.

Did he mean that?

She wrinkled her nose. She *wasn't* perfect.

'I don't know about that—it was okay. I didn't think there was anyone in here. Have you only just come in?'

Please have only just come in.

'I was already here when you came in.'

'Oh…' Her heart sank.

'It's been a hard day; I was just having five minutes.'

'In the dark?'

He was dressed now in jeans and a tieless inky blue shirt, which matched his eyes perfectly. He was no longer clean shaven, due to the late hour, and dark stubble shadowed his lower face, giving him a raw, masculine look. She wanted to touch it.

'You should've said you were here.'

'I wanted to listen.'

'To me? Why?'

He should have made it known he was there. Anyone else would have. It was only polite.

'I was curious.'

'I thought I was alone.'

She'd never have abandoned herself to the song as she had if she'd known he was there. Suddenly feeling naked before him, she instinctively crossed her arms over her chest.

'I didn't want to interrupt you.'

He was smiling at her. Not in that designer after-shave advert way he often used, but in a somehow softer way. In a way that made her feel as though she needed to sit down and take the weight off her suddenly buckling knees.

She crossed her arms more tightly. She wasn't being taken in by another handsome face and dazzling smile. He'd crossed a boundary. He should have spoken up.

'I wish you'd said you were there.'

'Well, I'm glad I didn't.' He sounded unremorseful. 'I'm glad I stayed where I was.'

'Hiding in the dark like some kind of spy?'

He'd known she'd thought she was alone—he must have. He hadn't made his presence known.

How dare he?

He'd spied on her, exposed her, judged her...

'More like a scout.'

She stared at him. 'A *scout*? A Boy Scout?'

He laughed. 'A talent scout.'

This wasn't happening.

She needed to leave. He was making fun of her. 'I should get home...get something to eat. I'm back at seven in the morning.'

'You haven't eaten? Me neither. Let's get something together. My treat...to apologise for being a spy.'

She didn't want to. In fact, she wanted to run. She wanted to be back in the safety of her home.

Away from him. So she could work out how she was going to face him again.

'Please… Come on—we're both tired and hungry. There's a great pizza place just down the road. You look as though you could eat a pizza.'

He turned and began to walk back down the aisle towards the chapel door, picking up her fleece and bag, offering them to her and waiting.

He was right. She was tired, and hungry, and she knew for sure that she looked like a girl who enjoyed pizza. A little too much pizza—most of which sat on her well-rounded, apparently child-bearing hips, according to her mother. And she'd have to face him tomorrow anyway, so why not just tough it out tonight?

'They do an amazing margherita,' he said.

She sighed. She couldn't undo what he'd seen and heard, could she? And the floor wasn't going to open up and swallow her.

The rich, jewel-coloured stained glass window behind him cast shafts of ruby, emerald and sapphire onto him, making him look as if he'd been sent from heaven. She walked towards him, head held high, taking the fleece and her bag from his hands as she passed him.

'You're paying.'

Max had known even as he'd been doing it that he shouldn't have sat silently at the back of the hospital chapel in the dark, watching her. When Lois had walked in he'd expected her to light a candle, or sit for a few moments and then leave. But then she'd put on the altar lights, stood centre-stage and appeared to be about to perform. That had probably been the moment to admit he was there, but the need he'd felt to hear her had overridden the knowledge that he should speak up.

He was glad he'd stayed quiet. Her voice was amazing—exquisite—and he definitely wanted her to perform in his show. But he had the distinct impression that she wasn't too pleased he'd watched her—and really, she was right. But he'd been sitting there on his own, in the dark, and he didn't want to explain the reason for that to anyone.

The pain of William's death was with him every day, but today he felt it even more so. Perhaps other people in similar circumstances would have spent time with family, but that port of call had been denied him for a long time. And so he'd found his way to the little chapel to be alone in the darkness. And he didn't want to have to answer any questions about why that was.

'So, why *were* you sitting in the dark, spying on me?'

They'd walked the short distance to the restaurant, making small talk about the warmth of the summer evening and how it was easy to forget the passing of time when on shift and end up working over.

Now Max chose a table in the corner, beside a wall with a painted fresco of an Italian courtyard scene, complete with pencil-thin cypress trees in terracotta pots. The waiter came over to take their order, replacing the almost burnt down votive candle in its crimson glass jar, lighting it with a long taper.

'I wasn't spying.'

He sort of had been.

Lois dipped her bread into the dish of olive oil and brought it to her lips, but stopped short of biting into it. She looked at him, long-lashed emerald eyes gazing into his own, brim-full of irony but still exquisite.

'Okay, I'll rephrase that. Why were you watching me covertly in the chapel instead of politely making your presence known, as most people would have done?'

She bit into the bread, the oil glossing her lips. She was definitely not happy with him but he wasn't going to explain. He didn't want her pity. But he did want her to sing.

'It's a good place to just sit and catch your breath after a trying day.' He wasn't lying. He wasn't telling the full truth either—but how could he? 'How's the bread?' he asked.

She dabbed her lips with a napkin, ignoring his question. 'Why the chapel? Are you religious?'

Not after what he'd been through. No benevolent deity would put anyone through that.

'No. It's just the chapel is about the only place in the hospital where there isn't chaos, noise and someone who wants something from you.'

And that had been exactly why he'd gone there today—even if it was an odd place to be on the evening of your birthday. But he'd needed somewhere quiet to think about William, his twin, who ought to be sharing his birthday with him but hadn't in more than two decades.

For over twenty years their birthday hadn't been celebrated…at all. In fact, celebrations of any kind had stopped the moment William had died. No more birthdays…no Christmases…no graduation celebrations. The contrast between how life had been and how it had become was so extreme it wouldn't have been believable if he hadn't seen it with his own eyes.

'Margherita for two?'

The smiling, dark-haired Italian waiter placed a huge pizza between them both.

Lois looked from the pizza and back to Max with wide eyes. 'You were right…that one is enough for two. Although I haven't eaten since having an early lunch, so if pushed I could manage it all.'

She smiled at him apologetically and he didn't want to look away.

"Tuck in then," said Max. But Lois had already taken a slice and groaned with pleasure as she bit into it. "Good?"

"Mmm," she replied, covering her mouth with her hand, "really good but don't let me have it all. You've been here before then?"

"Too often," he said with a grimace, lifting a large slice from the stone and stretching the cheese until it broke. "It's way too handy to nip into on the way home and I'm not a cook so I do rely on it a little more than I should."

"Only the Italians can do pizza as well as this." She took another slice, wrapping the stretched out cheese around her finger and popping it into her mouth. "Just what I needed."

'I can order another if you're hungry?'

'Noo.' She patted her hips and sighed. 'I can't afford the calories.'

She was perfect.

What was it with women and calorie-counting? He'd never understood the need some women had to be stick-thin. It was both unhealthy and unattractive.

'You don't need to worry about calories. Anyway, you're an opera singer—you *should* be voluptuous.'

His breath caught in his throat.

How had that come out the way it had?

Picking up his wine glass, he took a mouthful of the chianti, barely registering the taste.

Had that sounded like flirting?

Damn it.

'I'm going to get a coffee—do you want one?' he asked.

If she responded to his unwitting compliment and flirted back he'd have struggled not to continue it, and that would have been a dangerous game to play. But Lois wasn't a typical wannabe moocher, looking for a free ride into TV. She was a complete professional who was probably already happily partnered up with some lucky guy.

And that thought unsettled him more than was comfortable. There was no wedding ring, though—he'd checked that earlier and berated himself for doing so.

'I'm okay, thanks.'

Pushing the plate away from her, she placed her folded napkin onto it and zipped her hospital fleece up to her neck.

'I should get home.'

She wasn't looking at him. Something had changed. Had she thought he was flirting? If she had, she clearly didn't welcome it. She'd suddenly closed herself off.

Damn it, why had he said that? Voluptuous? Really?

"Have another slice." He nodded towards the pizza.

"I'm done…thanks."

'You've got time for a quick coffee.'

The waiter came over, having noticed Max raise his hand to beckon him. 'Two coffees, please. An espresso and… Lois?'

He was stalling—trying to keep her there for a bit longer.

Why?

To figure out the right moment to ask her about the show?

Because he liked looking at her?

Because this was the best birthday he'd had for a long time…even if he wasn't going to explain that to her?

She opened her mouth to speak, then hesitated and sighed. 'I'll have a decaf, please.'

Good.

But looking at her made him want to pull his

chair in closer…find out why she'd suddenly closed up…look into her eyes.

That was a very bad idea. He had a mission he needed to accomplish. Years in the making, now it was near to completion, and he needed to finish it in as short a time as possible. Staying in London— where he'd grown up, where he'd ruined lives—had been a test of endurance. Aged twelve, he'd had no choice but to stay, even if his parents had been so buried under the weight of their own grief, and consumed by the blame they'd put on him, that he was all but shunned.

He'd run away once. It had been the first anniversary of William's death and facing them, seeing their pain and feeling so responsible for it, had been more than he could bear. He'd been found the next morning by the owner of the boathouse he'd slept in by the river and taken home. When his father had died, later that year, his mother had told him he'd died from a broken heart, making it clear in no uncertain terms that Max was responsible for his father's death too.

Growing up, becoming a heart surgeon had seemed like the natural thing to do, and it had at least given him a sense of purpose. Perhaps by saving other people he could in some way make up for the deaths of William and his father. Maybe even make his mother proud of him. But that had always been nothing but a vain hope. And not everybody could be saved—however hard he tried. Knowing that was a reality he hadn't yet learnt to live with. And being unable to deal with losing a patient gave him tunnel vision—nothing else mattered. Not how he spoke to people, not how hard he pushed the boundaries, not the risks he took.

And that was why Lois thought he was a puffed-up prat.

'You really do have a beautiful voice,' he ventured.

He had to change her mind about him. He needed her to sing.

'Are you classically trained?'

She wrinkled her nose in that completely endearing way and he couldn't help but smile. It was becoming a habit.

'No, just the church choir—since I was about eight years old.'

Her lips curved into a cautious smile, and suddenly tearing his gaze away from them was impossible. He wanted to brush his own lips against them…feel the fullness of them.

What was she doing to him?

Lowering his gaze, aware that the beating of his heart had suddenly intensified, he tried to find words which didn't include *I want you*.

'You could be a professional,' he told her.

The caution in her smile gave way, and suddenly that sexy assuredness was back, shining out of her. 'I a*m* a professional.'

'A professional *singer*.'

'A professional nurse is all I want to be.'

She reached for the sugar at the same moment he did and his fingers almost touched hers. She snatched her hand away as though she'd touched hot coals and placed her hands in her lap under the table.

So near and yet so far…

Stop it. And ask her.

'I'm doing a show…for charity.'

She looked at him warily, her emerald eyes narrowed.

'No.' She crossed her arms.

'You don't know what I'm going to say yet.'

'I think I do.'

She was right; but he wasn't going to accept her answer. He wanted her at the show. She'd be sensational—and he needed to sell way more tickets to make the kind of profit the fund needed.

'It's for charity,' he said again.

'I know. I've seen the posters. But I only sing in church.'

'You'd be the absolute star of the show.'

She sighed heavily, picked up her discarded napkin and refolded it, not looking at him. 'Don't be ridiculous; Pathology are doing their magic act, Roman from Accounts is fire-eating, and the guys from Ophthalmology are doing their Take That tribute. I can't compare to that.'

'People would pay good money to see Sister Newington dressed like an opera diva and singing like a nightingale—I certainly would. Please.'

'No.'

'It's for charity.'

'That's below the belt.'

'To help save babies…'

'Stop it!'

'At least you're smiling now.'

She was, and even though she was clearly trying to suppress it, it was beautiful and it made her green eyes sparkle.

'You know you want to.'

'You're incorrigible.'

'It has been said…'

She drained her coffee and disappointment flooded through him—the evening was almost over. But spending longer with her would be a dumb idea. The more he spent time with her, the more he found she intrigued him. Why would someone with a voice like that be so reluctant to share it? He couldn't leave it there—he had to have her in the show.

'Is it a religious thing?'

'What do you mean?'

'Is it that you only perform in church and nowhere else for religious reasons?'

'No.'

'Then why won't you sing at the show?'

She sat up straight, tilting her chin. 'I don't need a reason.'

The defiance in her tone told him she wanted to end this conversation.

'I should get back. Thank you for the pizza.'

But he didn't want to end it—not until she'd agreed to be in the show.

'Lois, please… At least think about it—I really think people would enjoy it.'

He had to get over the line with this fundraising. The sooner he did that, the sooner he could leave London. His home city had gone from being a colourful, vibrant, happy childhood home into a place of dark, painful memories. He needed to get away from it. And if he could make good on his promise, that was exactly what he was going to do.

California was five thousand miles away—far enough for him to get away and maybe start a new life. And that meant not getting involved with anyone.

She stood and shrugged her bag on to her shoulder. Suddenly it was imperative that she saw how important this was.

'Lois, please. Sit down again and just listen for a moment. Let me explain the problem I have.'

Stunning emerald eyes held his, and it was all he could do not to forget what he wanted to say. But this was important—his life's work. And if he didn't succeed… Well, that wasn't even worth thinking about. It would be years of building his career, honing his skills, making the right connections, making promises, for nothing. It not working out wasn't an option.

She sat down again and placed her bag on the back of her chair.

He took a breath. This was for William, and for his twelve-year-old self who'd failed to save his twin when he'd suddenly collapsed as they'd played in the garden of their home over twenty years ago.

'You know that I want to launch the first trial of an aortic valve disease screening programme?'

'Yes. The posters are splashed all over the hospital.'

'It's taken me years to get agreement to run the trial and it means everything to me...everything, Lois. I have agreement in principle to run it, but I have to raise the funding...by the end of the month. If I don't, the deal is off and the Department of Health will cancel the trial. This screening programme will save lives, and I really believe that adding your name to the posters will sell more tickets to the show.'

He hadn't meant to reach out and touch her arm, but when he realised he had, and that she hadn't moved her arm away, he knew something had changed between them. He didn't want to, but he removed his hand.

'Sorry.'

Beautiful, intelligent green eyes searched his. 'It's okay. This clearly means a lot to you.'

'It means everything.'

The need to reach out and touch her again was almost overwhelming. She had to see he was genuine and serious. He didn't just want to *trial* the screening programme—he wanted to roll it out across the whole country. He had to. No one else should have to go through what William's death had put their family through, and it was his responsibility to ensure that. But he wasn't going to give her that last piece of information. He didn't want her pity.

'And they really might cancel it?' She said the words as though unable to believe them.

'They check where the donations come from. I can't just put the money in myself. It has to come from genuine donations.'

'I didn't realise there was any risk it wouldn't get off the ground.'

'It has to get off the ground.'

It had to for William.

She held his gaze, concern etched on her brow and shining from her eyes.

And suddenly she changed. Taking a slow breath, she sat up straight, her lips set in a hard line. 'Well, we can't have that can we? Okay, I'll do it.'

His heart leapt. 'You will?'

'Only one song, though.' She spoke sternly but her smile was playful.

'Whatever terms you like, Lois. I just want your name on the posters and you on that stage.' It felt entirely natural to grasp her hand now. 'Thank you.'

'I just hope you don't regret it.' She lowered her eyes, slipping her hand from his and reaching for her bag.

'I won't.'

She pushed her chair back and he stood too.

'Can I give you a lift home—it's late.'

'My car's only round the corner, but thanks.'

He didn't want her to go. 'See you tomorrow?'

'I'll be on the unit first thing.'

Fighting the urge to go after her, he watched her leave. Never had a woman filled his senses like she did. Never had he wanted to touch someone so badly. And never had he let his guard down, even if it had only been a little.

He needed to get a grip.

He might well want Lois Newington, but there was no way he was going to allow himself to go there.

Cool it, Templeton.

He lifted his hand for the waiter. 'The bill, please.'

His reason for being at St Martin's didn't include falling for a woman. Falling in love wasn't in his repertoire. Hell, he'd spent his life making sure he *didn't* fall in love. His propensity to ruin lives meant that people were better off not having him around. Short term, no strings was more his style. And now he didn't even have time for that. His mission here was more important than anything else. Persuading Lois to sing at the show was simply a means to help him achieve his goal…

Wasn't it?

Wanting her in any other way was just a distraction he didn't need, and he had to figure out a way to clear all thoughts of her from his mind. Lois had said yes, and although that in itself created new problems, suddenly reaching the fundraising target was a real possibility, and his long-held need to leave the ghosts of the past behind him was within his grasp.

CHAPTER FOUR

'SHALL WE DO a round?'

Her breathing quickening even at the sound of his voice, Lois looked up from her desk. Max was dressed for clinic rather than for Theatre, wearing an immaculate dark blue suit, the jacket of which he was now removing. He hung it on a hook behind the door, reaching up, causing the white shirt he wore to strain against the well-defined angular muscles of his broad back. As he moved, he disturbed the air in the small office and his scent swirled around the room...fresh, aquatic, making her want to inhale deeply and take him in.

'Sure. All your patients have been fine overnight.'

She'd eventually fallen asleep last night still thinking about him, and woken up at three a.m. in a complete panic, having dreamt she'd appeared on stage at his charity concert naked.

She couldn't do it—just the thought of being on stage in front of people made her queasy.

Why on earth had she agreed to it?

Because she'd heard his brother had died from a failed aortic valve years ago, and she'd seen how much the screening programme meant to him.

When he'd reached out to touch her hand, his words tumbling over themselves as he'd explained about the funding and how the programme might fail at the last hurdle, he'd exposed a different side to himself. The super-confidence had vanished, just for a moment, and she'd had a glimpse of something that somehow seemed more real. Was there a deeper side to Max Templeton? One he usually kept to himself?

'Shall we go and see them?'

Lois stood and straightened her uniform dress, adjusting the silver buckle and the skirt, which had ridden up when she'd been sitting. Ridden up over her apparently *voluptuous* operatic frame.

His description of her figure last night had cut her. She wasn't quite as resilient to those kinds of comments as she'd thought she'd become, clearly. It really didn't matter that he didn't find her attractive. He didn't have to shove her size in her face, though, did he?

'Ready?'

His eyes flicked up from her waist and met her own as she looked at him, one dark eyebrow moved very slightly upwards, and he visibly checked himself when she met his gaze, straightening his features, as if she'd caught him doing something he shouldn't. He was probably comparing her to the glamorous women from TV Land whom he usually worked and played with.

'Let's go.'

She slipped past him and out into the hubbub and the busyness of the unit. She was happy with how she looked, and if Max Templeton wasn't, that was his look-out. She was done with feeling the need to conform to the socictal belief that to be attractive you had to resemble a super-thin catwalk model.

Emilio had spent most of their six months together telling her, in one way or another, that her mother had been right—she was plump and she was plain.

Why had she believed his lies when they'd first met?

He'd been sweetness and light at first, and she'd felt flattered—for the first time in her life—and had allowed herself to be seduced by his obviously empty compliments.

How could she have been so naïve?

Had she been so desperate to hear someone tell her she was attractive that she hadn't been able to see through him?

She took a deep breath, wincing at the memory of how easily she'd been sweet-talked into bed. And then the insinuations about her size had started— at such a low level that she hadn't really noticed them at first.

'No dessert for her!' he'd say to waiters with a smirk.

'Breathe in!' as he took photos.

And, *'I expect your prefer holidays in cold places, where you can cover up, rather than beach holidays?'*

His jibes had become increasingly barbed and cruel as time had gone on, but they had been so in-sidious she hadn't seen the level it had got to. But then, her mother had normalised body-shaming jibes, hadn't she?

Oddly enough, the last straw with Emilio had come even before she'd discovered his secret—that he had a wife and little daughter back in Italy. The last straw had come when he'd taken her shopping and insisted on buying a teeny-tiny dress she could never have hoped to fit into, laughing with the shop assistant and saying that he'd lock away the biscuit tin until it fitted.

Even months later, recalling that stung. And recalling it only reinforced the knowledge that she wasn't going to get up onto that stage next week and be judged by anyone else.

She wished she hadn't bumped into Max Templeton in the chapel—then she wouldn't be in this mess.

Let's see the patients, and then somehow I'll tell him I can't do the show.

'I spoke to the printers first thing, by the way,' said Max, following her, 'and they're going to reprint the posters for the show this morning.' He checked his watch. 'In fact, they should have done them by now. They said they'd deliver them by lunch, and I've asked my secretary to organise having them put up around the hospital asap.'

She turned around and watched him as he folded up the sleeves of his white shirt and tucked his tie through a gap in the buttons.

Stay professional, Lois—do not swear.

'That was quick.' Her voice had gone up an octave.

'I didn't want to give you time to change your mind.' He grinned and walked past her, heading for his first patient.

Oh, God. Now what?

Following him, she felt her mind whirling.

You'll just have to do it.

I can't.

He's left you no choice.

Damn him.

'Good morning, Mr Swain,' said Max. 'Mind if I check your pulse?'

His patient smiled. 'You can do anything you like to me, Doctor, after the miracle you've performed.'

Max smiled, placing practised fingers on his patient's wrist. 'It wasn't just me—it's a team effort.'

Big of him! And a little unexpected...

'They're all wonderful here,' Jack Swain agreed. 'Especially this one.' He smiled and nodded towards Lois. 'A proper angel, she is…can't do enough for you.'

'So I hear,' replied Max, looking at her with that eyebrow raised once more, awakening the butterflies. 'How are his numbers, Sister?'

'Numbers are good.' She didn't need to check the chart. 'Norad is off.'

The butterflies had commenced their dancing.

'Perfect. That means you're holding your own, Mr Swain. If you behave yourself, we should be able to discharge you to the ward tomorrow.'

Mr Swain gave a thumbs-up and Max turned his attention to Lois as they moved towards the next patient.

'Rehearsals start tomorrow night—seven p.m. in the lecture theatre. We can't rehearse in the Savoy itself as the ballroom is in use for a wedding.'

'Actually, I wanted to talk to you about that…'

'How's Mr Ferns been overnight? Recovering from the impromptu thoracotomy from yesterday?'

He was ignoring her. Almost as though he knew what she was going to say. Well, okay, it could wait. It wouldn't change her mind. The other acts were brilliant—he'd get the money he needed without her.

'He's been stable. Bloods show his clotting is normal; we've been titrating the heparin accordingly.'

Max glanced at the obs chart. 'I'm going to keep him on the ventilator for another day. Blood gases are pretty good, but I want to rest him after reopening his chest.'

Moving to the patient's bedside, he placed his stethoscope in his ears, bending to listen, then tugging the earpieces out and draping the instrument back around his neck.

'All sounds fine. Any concerns from you?'

Plenty. Mainly that I can't stop thinking about you. Also that I wish I hadn't agreed to be in your show.

'No, he's been behaving himself.'

'Just Luke Evans left for me, then, I think.'

How to tell him?

'We extubated him this morning and he's doing well.'

Luke Evans was sitting up in bed sipping water as they approached. He winced as he swallowed. He was indeed doing well, considering it had only been three days since the horrific road traffic collision which had given him, amongst other injuries, a punctured lung and an aortic tear—often fatal, and almost costing him his life.

Lois smiled and he looked up. 'How are you, Luke? Throat a bit sore?'

He nodded, placing the small glass of water back on his bed table.

'The breathing tube that was in your throat can cause a bit of soreness, but keep sipping at the water and it'll be fine. You're doing really well. How's your pain?'

She really felt for Luke. He was the same age as her and very nearly hadn't survived the horrific car crash. Driving home from work, he'd been hit by another driver who'd been high on drugs. His car had gone under the cab of a truck and been dragged along until it had come to a stop. He'd broken five ribs—one of which had pierced his left lung—his aortic arch had been torn, and his left leg had sustained open fractures which had required pinning and plating. The torn aorta had been enough to kill him and almost had. Only the speed with which the air ambulance had delivered him to hospital, eight units of blood and the skill of the surgeon standing beside her now had saved him.

It brought home just how a life could be changed or lost in the flash of a moment. And just how good Max Templeton was at his job.

'I'm a bit sore, but alive.' He managed a small smile, but talking made him cough and he winced.

'I'm hoping to be out of here in time to see the doc's show next week.'

He nodded towards Max, grinning, and her heart sank.

Why had she agreed to it?

She hated letting people down.

Max slid his stethoscope from around his neck. 'There's every chance of that—and even more incentive now, as Sister Lois has agreed to perform too.'

His stethoscope was in his ears before she could reply. Luke opened his mouth to speak but Lois hushed him with a finger to her lips. Speaking would cause him to cough, and prevent Max from being able to hear his chest properly. Besides, she was still working out how to tell him she wasn't doing it any more.

'Chest's clear.' He pulled the stethoscope from his ears. 'The chest drain can be removed later, as long as there's no more drainage, and we may be able to step him down to HDU. Keep up the good work, Luke. I'll see you later.'

'I'll bring some ice chips for your throat,' said Lois, as they began to walk away.

'Thanks, Sister.'

She glanced to Max. It was now or never. 'About the show…'

But Max was looking straight ahead to where the doors of the unit had swung open. He smiled widely as Jay Vallini, a fellow cardiac surgeon, strode in.

Was she ever going to find the right moment to tell him?

'Jay, how are you?'

'Good, chief. Yourself?'

Lois liked Jay Vallini. He was a good surgeon, had been around for ever and the patients loved him.

'Good. Listen, I hear you need a bed for your stent chap this afternoon. I've got a young guy— three days post traumatic aortic arch tear, pneumo-thorax, smashed-up leg. Extubated this morning and doing well, but I just need to keep an eye on him for a bit longer before we send him next door. You okay hanging on for a bit?'

The older surgeon beamed at Max, smacking him on the shoulder jovially. 'Don't worry, chief, I've got a couple of minors I can bump up the list and do first.'

'Excellent,' said Max, 'Oh, and spread the word...' He nodded towards Lois, who was watching the scene with increasing incredulity—Max Templeton had just done something no other surgeon had ever done: got Jay Vallini to alter his theatre list. 'Sister Newington has agreed to be in the show next week.'

Jay Vallini unfolded the large poster he was car-rying, beaming and holding it up like a prize for all to see.

'I know. That's why I popped in—to see if it was true. It is, then?'

Lois knew her mouth had dropped open.

Max looked delighted. 'Oh, great, the posters have arrived. As I said...spread the word. We need to sell tickets.'

Lois watched as Daisy, one of the unit's nurses, arrived on the scene, followed by Tom.

'Oh, wow,' said Daisy. 'Put me down for a couple of tickets.'

'Never mind a couple,' said Tom. 'We need a job lot—I can feel a unit night out coming on.'

Max's famous smile lit up his face. 'You see, Sister?' There was more than a note of triumph in his voice. 'I told you having you in the show would sell it out.'

And with that he turned and left, and suddenly she didn't know if she admired him or loathed him. What she did know was that there was no way she could possibly get out of the damn show now, and the heart-racing, breathless panic of her dream last night sprang from its slumber and rushed like water from a burst dam through her veins.

Nausea swept through her and her legs felt as if they wouldn't support her. Singing in the back row of the choir, hidden from view by the collective comfort of the other choristers around her, was one thing—exposing herself to the scrutiny of colleagues…on her own, on stage…was way out of her comfort zone. That was something other people did—people with confidence in themselves… people who looked as if they should be on stage.

Not people like her. Not plain, plump Lois Newington, who couldn't even get a date for the school prom and whose only grown-up relationship had been with a lying, cheating narcissist. Again, she winced at the thought of him, and at the exquisite, embarrassing shame his lies had caused.

Emilio.

Even thinking his name gave her a bad taste in her mouth. The memory of when she'd caught him video calling his wife back in Rome and how he'd looked puzzled at her shock resurfaced, making her squirm inside. He'd had the audacity to say he'd thought she already knew he was married. It had been unbelievable.

'I have to get some ice chips for Luke.'

She needed to get away and headed for the kitchen with a plastic cup to collect the ice. Pushing open the door, her palm made contact with a large, brightly coloured poster advertising Max's show.

St Martin's Hospital Vaudeville Variety Show
Now featuring operatic sensation
ITU's very own
Sister Lois Newington!

Her legs wouldn't work, and she desperately wanted to run. Max Templeton had played a blinder. There was no way out of it now. She wanted to help the charity, but how on earth was she going to get up on stage on her own? For a start, she had nothing suitable to wear. Singing in church required simple choir robes, which covered a multitude of sins. Singing for this—what had he called it? *A Vaudeville Variety Show?*—was something entirely different.

Her phone vibrated in her pocket as she filled the plastic cup with ice chips from the machine. She pulled it out, glad of the distraction.

'Nat, I was just thinking about you,' she said.

Natalie had been the one to pick up the pieces when she'd discovered Emilio's other life in Italy. She'd been such a huge support when she'd felt so humiliated after he'd left and everyone had discovered the truth. That she'd been so desperate to hear the sweet nothings he'd so readily whispered into her ear to get her into bed that she'd allowed herself to be used by someone everyone else had seen straight through.

'We need to go shopping.'

Natalie's tone told her she was not to be argued with.

'Do we?'

'Unless you have a ballgown fit to wear for your stage debut hiding in your wardrobe, yes.'

'Oh, you heard.' Lois's heart, already in her stomach, sank further. Word really had got around.

'Toby texted me. I think it's amazing you're doing it, Lois. I'm a tad surprised, I have to say, but I'm so pleased. You'll be brilliant. But we do need to find you a fabulous dress. Are you still on a day off tomorrow?'

'Up to now, yes.'

'Right. Well, don't go putting yourself down for an extra shift; we have to hit the town.'

Suddenly, the whole nightmare seemed very real. She had to take the ice to Luke, but didn't want to go back onto the unit—she wanted to run a long way away and hide from every reality that had hit her in the last twenty-four hours. From the prospect of standing up on stage and singing to her colleagues in a vaudeville show to the realisation that she wanted Max Templeton.

She wasn't sure which scared her the most.

CHAPTER FIVE

THE BALLROOM AT the Savoy exuded elegance and opulence. Huge crystal chandeliers hung from the ceiling of the ornately decorated Edwardian-style room. Dining tables had been exquisitely decorated with fresh white linen, vases of summer flowers, pillar candles and gleaming cutlery. The famous London ballroom had cost a pretty penny, but the celebrity friends Max had invited would expect nothing less, and getting them to attend his fundraising event would reap rewards in much-needed ticket sales and donations.

This had to work. Everything depended on it.

He headed backstage to check everything there had been prepared as he'd instructed. The acts would be arriving in the next hour or so and everything had to be perfect for them. It was they who were making the show possible, after all, and he was grateful to each and every one of them. The work he'd put into fundraising over the last couple of years was hopefully about to pay off, and this generous group of performers were going to be treated like royalty for making this happen.

The corridor backstage was quiet, for now, and his footsteps on the wooden floor unnaturally loud. It was the calm before the storm of the arrival of the cast. Before the banter, warming up of voices, tuning of instruments and general getting ready noise that would ensue.

He'd instructed that each act should have their own dressing room, furnished with everything they might need. He'd even had gold stars attached to the doors with the performers' names printed on them. Names he found himself searching now as he walked along.

LOIS NEWINGTON

He stopped searching, his heart suddenly banging in his chest a little harder than it had been.
Would she turn up tonight?
Guilt pricked his conscience. She clearly thought he'd acted a little fast getting the posters reprinted last week, and apart from making one barbed comment about him being a fast worker had all but avoided him since. Part of him had wanted to tell her that if she wasn't sure about doing the show she could duck out, but a larger part of him just couldn't. That larger part of him wanted her to sing tonight—and it wasn't entirely because she'd make money for the fund. *He* wanted to hear her sing again. The reason why had nagged at him all week, but he'd stopped trying to kid himself that it was simply because she'd be sensational and would get the audience reaching into their pockets for donations.
She'd turn up, he was sure of it.
Wasn't he?
If she really wanted to get out of it she could suddenly find she had to stay on the unit to cover for staff who were coming tonight. But she wouldn't

do that. The concern he'd seen in her eyes in the restaurant when he'd inadvertently reached out and touched her hand told him she cared, and he was certain she'd hate to let the side down. But there had definitely been a reluctance too. So which was going to win tonight? Her need to do the right thing or that part of her he'd seen only glimpses of—those sudden, fleeting, quiet moments of reserve that caused her to close down and lose that exhilarating sassiness that made him forget everything else?

He needed her tonight. He just had to believe she knew it.

Lois sat in the dressing room in front of the brightly lit mirrors as the make-up artist dipped brushes into pots of eyeshadow, blush and powder, dabbing and smoothing colour onto her cheeks and eyelids.

Was this really happening?

Natalie had given her a pep talk last night, recognising that she'd been on the cusp of having a meltdown.

'You have the most amazing voice, Lois,' she'd said. 'Just pretend there's no one else there.'

'But there'll be no one to hide behind and three hundred people there.'

And Max Templeton.

'Forget them. Close your eyes if you have to. You're going to look sensational in that dress.'

Lois had rested her head on the back of the sofa, a groan escaping her lips. 'More Pavarotti than Celine Dion, though.'

Or mutton dressed as lamb, as her mother had described her when she'd left for the sixth form prom.

'Stop right there,' Natalie had said. 'I know you well enough to know you struggle with compliments—and no wonder after how that rat treated you. But hear this from someone who cares: in the shop on Saturday, when you put that dress on, even without your hair done and with no make-up, you looked beautiful. And you'll be stunning on that stage. I'm not going to listen to any counter-arguments you might throw at me so don't waste your breath. And forget Emilio—everything that ever came out of that man's mouth was a lie.'

And with that she'd put her fingers in her ears and sung, *'La-la-la... I can't hear you!'* making Lois laugh.

The hairstylist breezed in to the dressing room just as the make-up artist was finishing up and Lois glanced at the clock on the wall.

Seven-thirty p.m. She had until nine to wait for her turn.

'How are we doing your hair, Lois? Up? How about a few curls to frame your face?'

Her stomach lurched. This was getting more real and closer every minute.

'Just as it is, I think.' She didn't want to be accused of trying to make a silk purse out of a sow's ear.

'You do have gorgeous hair, actually. I don't really think you need me.'

Lois smiled at her. 'Thanks, it's about the only bit of me that doesn't need help.'

The hairstylist laughed. 'Well, you're the last one, so I'm done. Good luck tonight. It's a full house out there, you'll be pleased to know.'

Her stomach lurched again, and then once more at the sound of a sharp rapping on the dressing room door.

The hairstylist eased it open a little and peered round it. 'Hello…? Oh, hello!'

'I just wondered if Lois was there?'

Max.

Lois instinctively clasped the dressing gown she wore, pulling it more tightly around herself.

'Yes, she's here. But you can't come in—she's getting ready.'

Thank God.

'Oh, well, okay. Can you tell her to break a leg.'

'Pardon?' The stylist sounded horrified.

'Break a leg—it's a theatrical way of saying good luck.'

'Is it really?' She sounded doubtful. 'I'll tell her that.' And she closed the door, turning to Lois with a roll of her eyes. 'Did you catch that?'

Lois laughed. 'I did. And he's right—it's a way of wishing good luck before a show.'

'Stupid way of saying it, if you ask me. Perhaps it's a TV thing. Do you need a hand with your dress?'

Lois glanced at the gown she and Natalie had chosen at the weekend. It was indeed beautiful.

Simple in its design, but elegant. 'I'll be okay. Thanks for offering, though.'

She wanted a few moments before the final, decisive act of actually putting on the dress.

'Well, break a leg, then, I guess.' She nodded towards the dress. 'It's stunning. I'm going to see if I can sneak in at the back to watch the show. See you on the other side.'

She picked up her case and was gone, leaving Lois staring at a face she didn't fully recognise now that it had been painted and powdered, and knowing that, very soon, she'd have to put on a dress which would feel more than a little alien too.

There was another knock at the door. She froze.

'Lois?'

Max.

He tapped again.

Could she pretend she wasn't there?

The handle dipped.

'Don't come in… I'm getting changed!'

The handle moved back to its original position and she could breathe again.

'It's me—Max.' He spoke though the closed door.

I'm aware of that.

'I just wanted to check you're okay.'

'I'm fine, thanks.'

'And that you haven't run away.'

'I haven't…yet.'

'Don't say that. Everyone's really excited to see you on stage. Do you need anything?'

Just to be anywhere else.

'No, thanks.'

'Can I come in?'

'No, I've told you. I'm getting changed.'

There was a pause.

Had he gone?

'Okay.'

Another pause, but somehow she knew he was still outside the door.

'Lois?'

'Yes?'

'Thank you for doing this.'

She swallowed. This really did mean a lot to him, didn't it?

'You're welcome… But the same goes for this as goes for performing open heart surgery on my unit.'

'How's that?

'Don't make a habit out of it.'

Out in the corridor, Max Templeton smiled. He didn't understand why someone with such an amazing voice would shy away from public performance, but he knew that Lois did. He was grateful to her, as he was to all the performers who'd agreed to do the show, but he knew that Lois was doing it against her natural instinct not to. She was here, though, and the pangs of guilt he'd felt all week were now mixing in a heady cocktail with the anticipation of seeing her on stage.

He strode back along the corridor and into the ballroom, where the tables had now been cleared and the guests were mingling, drinking and chatting. Time to go back into host mode. Everyone here this evening was here because of him.

Because he'd asked them.

Because he needed them.

Years of work, planning, organising, talking to the right people, persuading, researching—all were culminating in this night. Tomorrow he had to go back to the committee in Parliament to tell them if enough money had been raised for the trial to go ahead. And if they finally signed off on the programme he would allow himself his reward—his new life in California as a non-practising professor, helping to train heart surgeons there. His new start.

Before that he would pay a rare visit to his mother. Rare because seeing his childhood home brought him face to face with the agony of what had happened there, and because he knew he wasn't welcome. But if the programme got the go-ahead he would walk back in and perhaps show that he'd done something good with his life—not made amends for what had happened, but at least done something positive—turned something that had been devastating into something to help others.

The hope that his mother might be able to forgive him had long since been obliterated, but there was still a chance that she might believe he'd achieved something to be proud of.

He straightened his bow tie. The nerves were real. This was for William.

And instantly he was twelve years old again. In the back garden, having a kick-about with his twin. Suddenly William had hit the ground before he'd seen it coming.

And Max had laughed. Breathless from running

around. Bending forward, his hands on his knees, catching his breath.

'Stop messing, Will!' he'd called. 'Just because you're losing.'

But William hadn't moved...

Max took a breath and strode to the nearest table. Picking up a jug of water, he poured a glass, taking a drink, and a moment to clear his mind. He had to paint on the smile that everyone expected... ensure they enjoyed the evening and reached deep into their pockets. Time for TV's 'Surgeon to the Stars' to make an appearance. Now wasn't the time for self-pity.

'Max!'

An ex-patient strode towards him, hand outstretched, beaming a bright white Californian smile. One of Hollywood's elite—an actor of high renown—last year he had flown to the UK to be treated by him.

'It's been too long, my friend.'

And so it began. Everyone was here for him, and he was there for William. And this time he wasn't going to let him down.

The atmosphere in the ballroom was one of joy, fun and energy. The acts so far had been excellent. But by nine p.m. Max had begun to wonder why he'd not put Lois first on the bill. No one had come to tell him she'd hightailed it out of there, but the longer time went on, the more he wondered if she might get cold feet.

Standing in the wings, straining to see through

the bright lights to the opposite side of the stage, where she'd make her entrance, he felt his heart beating way too fast for comfort.

She wasn't there.

Maybe she was just standing too far back behind the curtains.

Maybe the blinding brightness of the lights was the reason he couldn't see her.

As the last act exited stage left, to much applause, he took the microphone and strode out from the wings. A beam of spotlight hit him, following him as he strode to the centre of the stage—TV's most well-known doctor, smiling his famous wide smile, raising his hands and joining in the applause.

He lifted the microphone. 'Wasn't he amazing? How does he *do* that?'

Whistles and cheers demonstrated that the audience agreed with him.

The applause died down.

His heart rate notched up.

She had to be there.

There was no way of checking now. The show had to go on.

He stood in front of the microphone stand, every cell in his body hoping she was standing in the wings.

'Ladies and gentlemen, next up, for your delight and delectation, I am thrilled to introduce to you someone we all know as a consummate professional…someone who runs our hospital's intensive care unit with supreme skill…someone who cares for her patients and her staff with compassion, professionalism and superb talent—and someone who has a hidden gift which she's going to share with us tonight. So, without further ado—and for one night only—it gives me great pleasure to introduce to you... Lois Newington!'

The applause began again and Max held his breath, unable to see anything except the blinding bright light that was on him.

Was she there?

The applause suddenly grew louder and a stunning woman in a floor-length, dark forest-green velvet dress appeared from stage right.

Lois.

She was all he could see. Everything else—all sights, all sounds—faded into the background. It was her...but it wasn't. Her golden blonde hair was down, cascading around her bare shoulders. She walked towards him, eyes down, dark lashes fanned on her cheek, and he was sure he gasped as she raised those emerald eyes to look at him as she arrived centre-stage. They matched the dress perfectly, and when the diamond and emerald necklace she wore drew his eyes down to a deep, rounded cleavage, his body reacted in the most instinctive way.

Lifting his eyes to meet hers, he smiled, and his breath caught in his throat when she returned it. Not a beaming, showy, TV smile that a professional diva might grace him with, but a tentative one, a shy one, a brave one.

He turned, managing somehow to tear his gaze from her, and left the stage, handing the microphone to one of the stage hands. He wanted to see this properly—not from the back of a dimly lit chapel, not from the wings of the stage, but from the audience.

The strings of a guitar had already begun to play the first bars of the introduction to the song. The ballroom of this prestigious London venue was silent, save the haunting melody coming from the single guitar. The spotlight was on Lois, the most beautiful woman he'd ever seen, standing bravely, eyes closed, about to sing.

No one else was in the room.

Open those amazing eyes, Lois. Look at me.

And she did.

And it took his breath.

Could she see him? Or were those emerald eyes gazing out into the lights, dazzled by them, unable to see into the silent audience? Unable to see his captivation?

As she began to sing, and the first clear, pure notes left her lips, she lifted her eyes and they sparkled in the brilliance of the spotlights which had converged on her, illuminating her, making her the centre of everyone's attention.

He was lost. Her voice was ethereal...enchanting and exquisite. And she looked magnificent. Glossy golden waves framed her face and fell onto the creamy softness of her bare shoulders, drawing his eyes down to the velvet bodice of her gown, which tapered in at the waist and then flared over her hips, cascading to the floor. The melody was seductive, hypnotic—like being cocooned in a gently swaying cradle. He didn't want it to end. But he knew the end was coming.

Her breathing deepened as the song built to its crescendo, deepening the rise and fall of those tantalising glimpses of the porcelain curves of her breasts. Her eyes closed for the final notes and every inch of his skin prickled with goosebumps. He'd never hear that song again without remembering this moment. Nothing had ever connected to his soul like that.

The applause was thunderous. People were on their feet, clapping, whistling, cheering, taking stems from the flower arrangements on the tables and flinging them onto the stage. His heart soared. She couldn't regret doing this now. Surely even she could see this as confirmation of her talent.

His bleep vibrated in his pocket.

No!

He turned to Jay Vallini, who was next to him, cheering.

'I've been bleeped. Can you compere for me? The running sheet is with the guys up there in the wings.'

'Sure, chief, sure,' replied Jay. 'Hope it's nothing you need to go in for.'

They both left the room—Jay Vallini making his way onto the stage to help Lois pick up the flowers, and Max heading out to find a quiet corridor to call the hospital, desperately hoping it was something he could deal with over the phone.

CHAPTER SIX

HEART BANGING IN her chest, Lois almost ran back to the sanctuary of her dressing room. Placing the armful of flowers into the sink, she ran the tap and sank gratefully into the comfy armchair, resting her head back, trying to slow her breathing.

It was over.

The sharp rapping on the door made her jump.

'Lois?'

What was Max doing backstage? He was compering the rest of the show, wasn't he?

'Hello?'

'Can I come in?'

No! She needed to get her breath back.

'Lois? You're dressed now.'

She sighed, unable to think up a reason to decline, went to the door and opened it. A runner dashed past, the performer in the opposite dressing room came hurrying out and the loudspeaker made some sort of announcement.

Max stood looking at her, silently, and her insides, already frazzled by the night so far, began their butterfly dance.

'You were amazing.'

She lowered her eyes. Compliments were bittersweet—nice to get, but also a reminder of the huge error of judgement she'd made with Emilio.

'Thank you.'

'I just wanted to tell you that before I leave.'

'Leave? What about the rest of the show?'

'I've been called in. Luke Evans's chest drain has dumped five hundred mils in the last hour. I need to go and see him.'

'Is he holding his BP?'

'For now… He's young, though, so he's got reserve. But if it continues draining, he could crash.'

'I'm coming with you.'

There was no way she wasn't going to make sure Luke was okay.

Grabbing her black leather jacket, she practically pushed Max out of the door. 'Let's go. Where's your car?'

'Bike.'

For a moment she just looked at him, but then remembered they needed to move fast and closed the door behind her.

They set off down the corridor. 'You cycled here?'

'Motorbike,' he called back over his shoulder.

'Do you have a spare helmet?'

'Yes.'

He pushed on one of the revolving doors in the foyer, declining the taxi offered by one of the doormen.

Half running to the motorbike, Lois struggled to keep up with him.

Why hadn't she ditched the heels?

His helmet hung from one of the handlebars and he put it on, handing her the spare. Thankful she'd declined an updo from the hairstylist, Lois pulled the helmet on, fastening the chin strap. Then, gathering the full skirt of her dress into her arms, she put one leg over the seat and bunched the fabric in front on her.

Max turned. 'Hold on tight; we're not going for a Sunday drive.'

Lois reached around his waist, her heart hammering in her chest. It was only a couple of miles to St Martin's—in a straight line. But there weren't many straight lines in the middle of London. She had no choice but to hold on tight.

Max kicked the engine into life and it roared as he revved it. Leaning in close, resting her head on his back, her knees squeezing firmly against the seat, skimming his backside, Lois hung on for dear life.

But there was nothing scary about being nestled into Max Templeton's wall of a back…nothing to fear about resting her head against his broad shoulders, feeling his muscles move as he controlled the bike around corners. Nothing alarming about being so close to him that the warmth of his body spread into hers and his scent filled her.

As they chased through the streets of London, her body was forced to move with his as he tilted the bike around the curves in the road. She watched the light on the Thames shimmer as they sped across Waterloo Bridge to the south bank.

There was no fear for her safety. It wasn't fear that made her heart bang against her ribs so hard she felt sure he'd be able to feel it through both their leather jackets. It was desire. And holding on to him, moving in sync with him, fear wasn't what she felt. She knew only the exhilaration of the cool wind in her face and the thrill of being almost as one with him.

Max didn't notice the open-mouthed stares from the staff as he pushed open the doors to the ITU. He could still feel Lois pressed against his back, her arms around his waist, her knees gripping either side of his thighs. If he hadn't needed to reach the hospital asap, he'd have taken a longer route just to keep her close for longer.

But the familiar sights, sounds and smells of the ITU brought him back to reality, and his focus now was Luke Evans. He strode to his patient's bedside, leaving several staff members staring after him, their gaze only leaving him when Lois followed him in, green velvet gown skimming the floor, black leather jacket undone and her usually tied back hair loose around her shoulders.

'Hi, Luke, how are you?' he asked, also acknowledging the presence of Robert, one of the doctors on his team.

Luke's chest drain had been removed a couple of days ago, but he'd been readmitted to the ITU earlier with a swinging pyrexia and a new hemopneumothorax, which had required Max to replace the chest drain.

Luke managed a weak smile, but was obviously unwell.

'Well, we'd much rather be at the show,' said Robert. 'But you really didn't need to bring the show to us.'

Max looked down at his dinner suit and then to Lois, who stood at the end of the bed, scrutinising the obs chart. His stomach clenched.

Just look at her.

Even the incongruity of her looking like that in this setting couldn't detract from her beauty. In fact, it enhanced it—if that were possible. She hadn't thought for a second about leaving the show and coming with him to see Luke. She should be there now—enjoying the adulation she so deserved, hearing everyone tell her how amazing she was. But she'd chosen to put her patient first and he couldn't help but admire that, even though he felt guilty that she wasn't enjoying the rest of the evening as she should have been.

He shouldn't have told her where he was going.

She glanced up at him. 'I'll check to see if the microbiology report is available…back in a tick.'

He watched her leave, hitching up her skirt a little to save it from dragging on the floor, revealing the golden glitter of her shoes.

'Just going to check this drain, Luke,' he said.

He crouched beside the bed, inspecting the tubing and the contents of the bottle. He knew what his plan was for Luke. He was concerned, but they hadn't run out of options. Lois returned with an iPad and he stood to read the report.

'What's the damage?' asked Luke, a little breathless and with a slight frown creasing his forehead.

Max gave him a reassuring smile. 'Nothing a good dose of IV antibiotics can't sort out. The fluid which collected in the pleural space where the broken ribs were has developed an infection, but it's common in this situation so don't worry.'

Luke seemed to relax, pulling his oxygen mask from his face to speak again. 'Looks like it was a very glamorous evening.'

He nodded towards Lois, who was busying herself at the end of the bedspace, making notes on his chart.

Max returned Luke's smile. 'Very.'

She'd blown his mind tonight. Her voice had filled the ballroom with its purity and power and she'd filled his senses with her beauty and her courage, bringing surprising and uncharacteristic tears to his eyes that he'd had to swallow hard to contain. She had no clue what she'd done to him. She didn't realise the gift she had. She had no idea that all he wanted to do was take her in his arms.

'Will you want a fluid challenge?'

Lois was looking at him with the same emerald eyes that had met his on the stage, but now they held certainty and confidence rather than the brave fear he'd seen before her performance. She was back in her comfort zone.

'Let's give a litre of normal saline over two hours and we'll get a chest X-ray too, please.'

She lowered her gaze, tapping on the iPad.

She hadn't let him down, despite her reluctance. She'd come to the ball like Cinderella. Beautiful, brave and humble. She should be enjoying her moment back at the Savoy, hearing how people loved her performance, getting the affirmation she deserved.

'Do you want me to review the X-ray when it's done so that you can get back to the show?' asked Robert. 'It's only ten o'clock, so there's time to get back before it finishes.'

He was right—there was time to get back. Time to get Lois there and allow her to see the impression she'd made. But he didn't want to leave Luke.

'Get Cinders back to the ball before midnight strikes,' said Robert with a grin.

It wasn't very often that he didn't know instinctively what to do, but he was torn. He wanted to make sure Luke had his first dose of antibiotics and review the X-ray. But he also badly wanted to take Lois back so she could hear the praise everyone undoubtedly wanted to lavish her with.

'I can call you with the X-ray result,' said Robert.

'Go,' said Luke.

'I can send the X-rays to your phone, if you like,' added Robert.

They were talking sense. So why did this present such a difficult dilemma?

'We don't have to go,' said Lois. 'I've already done my bit on stage. Let's get the antibiotics up and see what the X-ray shows.'

And suddenly he could make the decision. She'd read him. She'd seen his reluctance to leave, understood, and was giving him permission to stay. Admiration for this woman filled him—warmed him and swelled in his chest. She got his need to put the patient first every time, above all else, because that was what she did too. But she'd also made him realise that he wanted to put her first.

'Thanks, Robert, I appreciate it.' He turned to Luke. 'You're in good hands. I'll see you tomorrow.'

Luke gave him a thumbs-up.

Taking the iPad from Lois, Max handed it to Robert. 'Come on, let's get back—make sure all those celebs have dug deep into their pockets.'

'But…' began Lois, her hands empty but still in position as if she were holding the iPad.

'Go,' said Robert. 'I'll text Max the results.'

Max held the door open for Lois and she looked from one to the other of them.

Max swept his palm towards the door. 'Let's get you back to the ball, Cinderella.'

'I really don't need to go back,' said Lois as they headed off down the corridor, past where the Saturday night walking wounded were spilling out from A&E.

'You really do,' replied Max, ignoring with accustomed ease the stares and whispered comments from people who'd recognised him.

Lois shot him a sidelong glance which told him she required an explanation.

'I sense you don't cope with compliments very well,' he began, pushing the button on the wall to open the exit to the hospital. 'But I think you need to hear that people loved your performance tonight. I wish I hadn't told you I was leaving. I pulled you away from what should have been your evening. So I'm taking you back…to your admiring audience. So that you can hear for yourself that you were amazing.'

He pulled his helmet on and grinned at her through the visor.

'Come on, then; before this bike turns into a pumpkin.'

Lois gazed dismally at herself in the dressing room mirror. Whoever had designed the motorbike helmet had clearly not given much thought to what it did to your hair. But holding on to Max as they'd taken only a slightly more sedate ride back to the hotel had been worth getting mussed-up hair for. Ten minutes when she'd been allowed, almost been given permission to melt into him, to hold on to him tightly, grip the tops of his thighs with her knees, feel his warmth, inhale him.

He'd been reluctant to leave Luke and she understood why. He cared for his patients, and she got that and admired it completely. But Robert and the rest of the team were more than capable of looking after him and it had been safe to leave when they had. Besides, it was preferable, really, that he got back to his show. He was the main attraction—the reason everyone had turned out and paid good money to be there. She'd wanted it to be his decision, though—which was why she'd given him a get-out if he'd wanted to take it.

But he'd wanted to bring her back so she could bask in the glory he felt she deserved.

Had he meant what he said? That people had enjoyed her singing?

He'd smiled…kindly…genuinely when he'd said it. He'd being paying her a compliment.

And he'd been right about that, at least—she *wasn't* good with compliments. What had led him to that conclusion?

Holding her head in her hands, elbows on the dressing table, she looked at herself in the mirror and frowned. The only compliments she'd ever had outside of the work setting had been from Emilio. And look what had happened when she'd believed *him*.

She sat up straight.

Don't be drawn into falling for another man's lies.

Going through that kind of humiliation again was not going to happen—not a chance. But Max clearly hadn't been about to take no for an answer and, floored by his apparently astute appraisal of her, almost without realising she'd found herself back on the motorbike, holding on to him as if he belonged to her, closing her eyes as she melted into him, feeling their bodies move as one and hot, breathtaking desire fill her once more.

She took a deep breath and looked at her reflection sternly.

'Stop it.' Picking up her brush, she dragged it through her dishevelled hair. 'He's only being nice because of the show.'

But her stern expression suddenly softened. He'd read her, though, hadn't he? Understood her. Seen the difficulty she had with compliments. The smile he'd given her through his smoky tinted visor had been warm, genuine. He knew something about her that few people did, and what he thought he knew seemed to matter to him.

Against the need he'd felt to stay with Luke, he'd made the decision to bring her back.

Why?

Because he felt she needed to hear that people had enjoyed her singing.

And that was thoughtful.

There was no other explanation.

The frown reappeared and she pursed her lips. There was definitely another side to Max Templeton. The problem was, that the more she saw of this kind, thoughtful, caring side, the harder it became to tell herself that he was just another overconfident, full-of-himself ass. And telling herself that was by far the safer option—it kept him away from her heart.

Picking up the lipstick Natalie had chosen for her, she slicked it onto her lips. Even if he did have some good qualities, she wasn't going to risk her sanity again by even thinking about allowing herself to fall for him.

She had to get back into the ballroom before it was all over and so, standing, she shook down her dress—which, remarkably, hadn't suffered from being gathered up around her knees for the bike ride. The velvet fabric was gorgeous, and Natalie had been right that the deep green was her colour. She didn't look bad, even if she did say so herself. The way the dress had been so cleverly cut gave her a waist she hadn't really known she had, and although the jewellery was only costume jewellery, it did complement her eyes as the shop assistant had suggested.

When she'd walked onto that stage earlier, her mother's words about being mutton dressed as lamb ringing in her ears, she'd hardly dared to look at Max as he'd stood centre-stage, looking like a film star in his exquisite satin-lapelled, tuxedo. But when she had, he'd met her gaze with a dazzling smile, and although she knew there were over three hundred other people in the room, his smile had seemed only for her.

But that was ridiculous. He was a showman. He'd spent more than enough time in front of cameras to learn how to seduce an audience and that was all he'd been doing. It was a show—that was all.

Walking down the corridor, past all the other dressing rooms with their golden, glittering stars, her golden, glittery stiletto heels click-clacking on the wooden floor, she put her shoulders back and lifted her chin.

And she could put on a show too.

For one night only, as he'd said, she was an opera singer.

Or Cinderella.

The fairy godmothers that were her best friend Natalie and Rebecca the make-up artist had waved their magic wands and helped her to do what she had to do. She'd already done the difficult bit, up on that stage, the rest would be a breeze in comparison. And then tomorrow she could go back to being Cinders—back to her comfort zone, back where she belonged. The glitz and glamour belonged to

those who wanted it—to those who looked the part
and felt comfortable in it. All she wanted was to be
back in her department, looking after her patients
and her amazing team of staff.

CHAPTER SEVEN

THE BALLROOM WAS buzzing with noise and activity. Everyone was mingling, chatting, drinking, schmoozing. Glasses were clinking, the DJ was in full swing, the odd cork popped off a bottle of fizz and there was a crowd on the dance floor, bobbing away to the music.

Lois recognised more celebrities than she'd expected: singers, actors, comedians, a few politicians. She took a deep breath. It was only an hour until midnight—that wasn't long, and the party wouldn't go on past then, surely. She could manage an hour.

A handsome male actor she recognised but couldn't remember the name of was smiling and walking towards her, holding out a glass.

'The opera star,' he said, approaching with a wide and very white smile. 'You don't have a glass in your hand. Here—we can't have that.'

He held out a glass of something with bubbles fizzing through it and Lois took it gladly, returning his smile.

'Thank you.'

'I have to say,' the man continued in conspiratorial fashion, 'I think you were the best performer this evening.'

'Oh,' replied Lois, 'well, I don't know about that, but thank you.'

'And you're a nurse?'

'Yes, that's my day job.' She took a sip of the very welcome ice-cold drink, the bubbles tickling her nose.

'You're a woman of many talents. You were sensational on stage tonight—congratulations.' He lifted his glass, smiling before taking a long drink. 'Like to dance?'

He lifted the glass from her hand and placed it with his own on a nearby table, taking her by the elbow and leading her towards the dance floor, where the DJ had switched from dance music to a slower number.

'I'm not very good at dancing.'

Lois didn't want to dance. She felt out of place. The ballroom was full of elegantly dressed, beautiful people. She didn't belong here.

He took her hand in his and gently placed his other hand on her waist. 'Don't worry, I'll lead. You'll be fine.'

She swallowed. He seemed nice, but people had started to look at them, making her heart rate climb as though she was back on stage. She managed a smile. He was one of Max's guests and would likely make a big donation. She couldn't *not* have a dance with him.

'I'll try not to step on your toes.'

Keeping her gaze firmly fixed on the man's black satin lapels, she answered his questions about her singing. It was only the sudden sound of Max's voice that told her he was standing beside them.

'Richard, old man—how the devil are you? I just

need to borrow Lois, if you don't mind...an urgent work matter.'

An excuse to leave the dance floor! Relief flooded through her, quickly followed by alarm. What had happened? Was Luke okay?

'Of course.' The actor released Lois. 'Thank you for the dance, Lois, and for not treading on my toes. Hope to see you again later.'

Max guided her away from the crowded dance floor and didn't let go of her elbow until he'd steered her out of the ballroom and into the large, equally opulent lobby.

'Sorry,' said Max.

'Is Luke okay? Did you get his X-ray result?'

He looked puzzled for a moment. 'Oh, yes...no.'

'Good.' She frowned. 'I think. So, what did you want me for? And what are you sorry about?'

His eyes had darkened to a shade she'd never seen before, and suddenly everything going on around them faded to nothing. He looked as if he was deliberating over something significant. Her breathing deepened. There was a tension between them. The air seemed to crackle...alive with tiny particles of fizzling anticipation.

'I'm sorry for breaking up your dance with Richard.'

It was more than that. What was going on?

The back of her neck prickled. 'That's okay,' she replied slowly.

'It was selfish of me.'

'It was?' She held on to the glass emerald at her

neck so tightly the edges of the facets dug into her fingers. She swallowed. 'Why?'

The power of his eyes was immense. She couldn't look away…didn't want to.

It was little more than a whisper, but his words were electrifying. '*I* wanted to be the one to dance with you.'

Max held out his hand towards her. She looked hesitant. She had every right to be, though, didn't she? He was well aware that he had a certain reputation with women. His celebrity status meant that the tabloids were always happy to print photos and make up stories about what they called his 'love life'. To be fair, the press stories about him had a grain of truth about them—he *was* a confirmed bachelor. But *love life*?

That was a little phrase they liked to trot out which meant nothing to him. He didn't have a love life. Love was an emotion he avoided like the plague. Love equalled pain, loss and grief. Lois, along with everyone else, was better off keeping well away from him and his reputation with love. Anyone he'd ever loved had, in one way or another, left him, been let down by him or rejected him.

He was steering well clear of love.

But she returned his smile and took his hand, her touch tightening every one of his nerves in an instant and weakening, with swift ease, his well-practised mantra not to feel anything.

'I think I can hear the opening strains of "Careless Whisper".' Her smile widened. 'I can never resist this one.'

Holding her hand, leading her back to the ballroom, through the mingling groups of guests to the softly twinkling dance floor, now packed with couples pressed together, he knew he was pushing his boundaries, trespassing into an unknown world…a world he'd never had any desire to venture into.

He felt things for Lois he'd never felt before. He knew what lust felt like, and although of course he desired Lois physically, there was much more to it than that.

What if this was how falling in love began?

Feelings? Caring about someone?

He smiled at people as they passed. Everyone seemed exactly as they had been before. No one else seemed to realise that the earth's tectonic plates had shifted slightly. Max Templeton was contemplating that what he was feeling might be mistaken as the first sign of something he most definitely didn't want to feel. And yet he was powerless to halt it in its tracks.

'May I?'

He moved his hand to her waist, but stopped short of touching her.

'You may.'

Her smile was shy, uncertain, but again there was bravery in her eyes. He held her waist and she placed one of her hands on his shoulder and the other in his. Pulling her closer, pressing her to him lightly, he gazed into soft emerald eyes which looked back at him, pulling him in, weakening his resolve to keep his distance.

Their race across London on the bike earlier, when she'd held on to him so tightly their bodies had almost moulded together had been exhilarating. Holding her now only confirmed that he wanted her.

So have sex and get it out of your system.

But it was more than that. He *felt* something. What that something was, he couldn't work out, but he knew it would take more than sex to find the answer.

Don't do this, Templeton. Stay back. Keep feelings out of this.

She looked up at him, a slight frown creasing her brow. 'I never really understood why this song has the power to bring couples to the dance floor—it's about heartbreak and being alone.'

'It makes *me* feel alone.'

His heart rate notched up. He knew which direction he was taking this. He was on dangerous ground, but this was travelling on one trajectory only. The need to kiss those lips was almost overwhelming.

'Does it?' she asked.

'Alone in this crowded room with you…everyone else has disappeared. Is that cheesy?'

Her eyes softened and her lips curved into a smile. His fingers ached to touch her face, to feel the softness of her cheek, the warmth of her full lips, now slightly apart, waiting to be kissed.

'Is it true?'

Emerald eyes glittered, daring him to answer truthfully.

Sassy Lois.

Undeniable lust shot through him.

'Yes.'

She took a breath, a moment to look into his eyes, as if to test his honesty.

So test it.

He *was* telling the truth.

'Then it's not cheesy.'

His breathing deepened. If this continued it could easily lead to them sleeping together. Did he want that?

Hell, yes. Look at her.

She was the most stunning woman in the room. And she felt amazing pressed against him. His palms ached for her.

And she'd sung for him.

Against her better judgement.

She'd strode straight out of her comfort zone and done this, tonight, for him. And even though she hadn't wanted to do it, she'd done it with style.

Every fibre of his being was grateful to her... admired her, wanted her.

Suddenly, there was no dilemma. To hell with not getting involved. He wanted Lois, and if she wanted him back, he'd deal with any fallout afterwards.

A weight lifted from his shoulders.

'You were amazing tonight. You looked stunning on that stage.'

And the glittering light in her eyes disappeared. Just like that.

His heart dropped like a stone to the pit of his stomach.

She dropped her gaze. 'I hope I did okay. I hope you get to the fundraising target you need.'

There was that vulnerability again.

He lifted his hand and touched her chin lightly, raising it, making her look up at him. 'You were much more than okay, Lois.' He wasn't flirting. He needed her to know how good she was because she really didn't know it. 'I'd say you stole the show.'

She smiled, but turned her head away. 'Thank you…that's kind. And thanks for indulging me with George Michael.'

The song had ended. The DJ was calling everyone to the dance floor for the final rousing tunes of the evening. It was nearly midnight. Cinderella was going to go home.

'I believe Max Templeton would like to say a few words before we end this amazing evening,' called the DJ. 'Where are you, Max?'

Max lifted his hand to acknowledge the DJ, then bent to whisper in her ear. 'In the words of George Michael…please stay.'

The crowd cheered and a spotlight lit up, following Max as he made his way to the stage to take the microphone. He had host duties to perform, people to thank, hands to shake, the last donations to be elicited.

He just hoped he could do all that before Cinderella disappeared.

* * *

Lois had shaken almost as many hands as Max had. People had been very kind, lavishing her with compliments on her singing.

'You were abso-flippin'-lutely brilliant,' said Natalie, hugging her as tightly as a heavily pregnant woman could manage.

'Amazing,' said Toby, planting a kiss on her cheek.

'I was so proud of you,' said Tom, clasping her. 'We all were. How come you kept that talent such a secret?'

'And Max was most definitely impressed,' whispered Natalie with a wink as she left.

Max.

He'd been flirting with her when they'd danced. And she'd let him. She watched him now, as he shook hands with the last few remaining guests as they filed out. Laughing, slapping some people on the back, planting kisses on the cheeks of others, flashing that famous smile from his handsome face. Charm personified.

Was it second nature to him as it had been to Emilio? Right up until she'd given in to his charms and he'd begun to change?

The actor Richard strode towards her, smiling and shrugging on his overcoat. It was as though she'd been parachuted into an after-show party at some Hollywood awards ceremony—she'd never seen so many celebrities all in one place.

'Well, I never got that second dance with you, Lois, but I can't say I blame Max for keeping you to himself.' He grinned as Max came towards them, slapping him on the back and shaking his hand. 'Great evening, Max. Well done.'

'Thanks so much for coming,' said Max. 'Good to see you again.'

Richard tapped his forehead, turned on his heel and headed for the door, calling to a concierge to get him a taxi.

'You made an impression there,' said Max, lifting his hand in acknowledgement as his famous friend disappeared through the revolving door.

'He was very kind,' she replied, registering Max's pursed lips and raised eyebrow.

What had Richard meant when he'd said Max had kept her to himself?

'Great evening, Max.'

Another glamorous couple approached and shook their hands.

'Good luck with the fundraising, darling,' said the woman, air-kissing his cheek, before she swept away. *'Ciao!'*

'Well, it looks as though we're the last ones standing.'

He glanced around the foyer. A few revellers sat around, still holding on to drinks, but most had left or gone to their rooms.

'I'll get my things from the dressing room and grab a taxi,' said Lois.

Was she glad the evening she'd so dreaded was actually over?

At least her nightmare of appearing on stage naked hadn't come true. In fact, people had been really lovely, and Max had been grateful—she'd seen it in his eyes when she'd walked towards him on stage. Yes, part of her was relieved the evening was over—the part of her that had spent most of her life believing she wasn't worthy of a night like this. But another, unfamiliar part of her would have quite enjoyed having more time to chat with people, dance with film stars and see Max look at her like that again.

Had he just been grateful…or had there been something else in his deep blue eyes? Those butterflies reawakened.

'I'll help you with your things and get a taxi organised,' said Max.

'Oh, don't worry. I can get a taxi myself—you must have loads to do.'

'I want to make sure you get home safely. Let me at least help you with your bags.'

The butterflies danced, pirouetting, twirling. Her instinct was to lower her gaze, but somehow she couldn't. Somehow his eyes held hers.

'Thank you, that's very kind.'

She didn't *need* his help…but she did *want* it. But it was simple kindness, wasn't it? He'd be making sure *all* the performers got home safely—helping *all* of them with their bags, not just her.

Don't kid yourself, Lois. You've fallen for all this before.

Maybe he had been flirting with her when they'd danced. But he'd been flirting with everyone this evening—he'd been playing the charming host. His job had been to make sure everyone had a great time and that they dug deep into their pockets for his programme. He'd told her she was amazing on stage, but he'd just been showing his gratitude—he'd have said that to everyone. It was his job.

He'd said she looked stunning too, and she'd almost believed him.

Almost.

Just in time, she'd remembered who she was.

Anyway, she didn't want to be lured into those enchanting eyes…lulled into the false sense of security his kindness could so easily invoke…enticed by his oh, so handsome face and toned, hard body. Life had taught her not to trust in those things. It only led to heartbreak and humiliation.

Most of the performers seemed to have left and the corridor was quiet. Lois pushed open the door to her dressing room.

'Did you hear yet from Robert?' She placed her hairbrush into her case.

Max stood on the threshold, filling the doorway. 'The X-ray showed a small collection in the left base, as expected—the antibiotics should sort it out.'

She zipped the case closed and attempted to lift it down from the table.

'Here, let me get that.'

Lois stood to one side so he could reach in and take the case, but the dressing room was narrow and his arm brushed against her breasts as he leaned over. The glancing connection shot electricity through her, making her breath catch in her throat.

He turned to face her, hypnotic blue eyes locked on her own. 'Sorry.'

She swallowed.

Why was he looking at her like that? How could he do what he was doing to her insides?

It had been the merest brush of his arm…the most casual touch…but her breasts fizzed as though he'd poured champagne over them. She fought not to lower her gaze—it was too good looking into those eyes, feeling the warmth of his nearness, inhaling the spicy aroma of him, enjoying just for a moment the pretence that he was about to take her into those strong arms…

And then he kissed her.

It was so sudden and unexpected that for a moment she froze. A squeak of shock caught in her throat, unable to escape because his lips were crushed hard against hers.

It was over in a moment.

She let out a breath. Her lips tingled, feeling suddenly swollen, warm, desperate for more.

'I'm sorry, I—'

But Lois cut him off.

'Don't be.'

He'd lit a spark somewhere deep inside her the first moment they'd met, and that kiss had thrown fuel on it, turning it into a blazing fire that wasn't going to be quenched without more of what he'd just given her a taste of. She didn't want to fall for

Max Templeton—but she didn't have to fall for him to have him kiss her like that again.

She could allow herself to be lost in the deep pools of his eyes…allow them to enchant her, hypnotise her, seduce her. She didn't have to fall for him.

'You're so beautiful, Lois…' His voice was a whisper. 'I couldn't resist. I don't know how I've resisted you all evening.'

Time stood still and she knew as she looked up into his handsome face that her lips had parted. He'd called her beautiful. She'd heard it before. From another man's lips. Another man who'd got her into bed and then changed into a narcissistic, cruel monster. No. Correction—Emilio hadn't changed. He'd always been a narcissistic, cruel monster. She just hadn't seen it.

So how could she be sure she wasn't making exactly the same error of judgement now? Emilio had taught her some harsh lessons. Lessons she'd promised herself to remember, learn from, never to repeat.

Don't trust.

Don't give your heart away.

Don't let anyone else crush you as he did.

She searched his face, looking for the truth.

There was honesty in his eyes.

Honesty.

And desire.

Heat flooded through her. Sometimes you had to cross your own boundaries. She'd done that already this evening, by getting up onto that stage, and that had worked out fine.

'I wasn't sure you were going to turn up tonight...'

His voice was low, edged with a seductive huskiness she hadn't heard him use before.

'When you walked out onto that stage you blew me away.'

He stoked her jawline with his finger and tilted her chin upwards.

He was going to kiss her again.

'You looked stunning.'

He ran his finger down her neck and across her collarbone, over the chain of glass diamonds and emeralds. She didn't move. Held in the power of his eyes, she didn't breathe. She didn't need to.

'And when you sang, I couldn't look away.'

Kiss me.

Her resolve had shattered. Her lips were begging him, tingling for the taste of him, and she had no intention of denying herself.

He wasn't Emilio.

And even if she wasn't the most beautiful woman he'd ever seen—as she clearly wasn't—it didn't matter tonight. Tomorrow was another day.

Rising up onto her tiptoes, she closed the gap between them. And although this time she was ready for it, when his lips met hers and she tasted him nothing else existed. Just the sweetness and the pressure of his mouth on hers...the warmth of his hands on her bare shoulders...the masculine scent of him filling her.

That was all there was.

All she needed.

Right up until the moment when he deepened the kiss, parting her lips with his tongue and groaning, pulling her closer. Close enough for her to feel his hard arousal through the velvet of her dress.

It was then that she wanted more.

CHAPTER EIGHT

HIS DECISION TO kiss her had been sudden, but not out of nowhere. He'd wanted her all evening. She hadn't been expecting it, though. She'd stiffened against him, and that was why he'd apologised and stood back.

What had happened between them then, when she'd looked into his eyes for what seemed like for ever, had happened without words…and without logic. He'd thought he'd overstepped the mark, misread the situation. But her eyes had softened, something had changed, and she'd been the one to reach for him. When their lips had met, much more softly this time, and she'd allowed his fingers to skim the porcelain softness of her neck, her kiss had assured him that she wanted this as much as he did.

But apart from sex, he had nothing to offer her.

He was on dangerous ground.

Why?

Because he'd stepped over the line—trespassed into a world he didn't belong in, one where feelings were allowed to run free with impunity.

And he didn't do feelings.

Besides, he was leaving, wasn't he?

'You know I'm only here for three more months?'

Emerald eyes stared back at him. There was a boldness in them he hadn't seen before and his stomach tightened.

'Yes, I was told,' she said.

Knowing that he wanted her wasn't news.

Knowing he might have her was something else.

But she deserved more than he could offer. Lois should be with someone who would love her deeply…be everything she ever wanted…give her children. Things that were pretty normal. But he couldn't do any of them. Anyway, in three more months he'd be five thousand miles away.

He didn't want to be in London. He'd stayed because it was where he'd needed to be to achieve what he wanted. As soon as the screening programme was over the line, he was leaving. His new position was all lined up, and the faraway sunshine and freedom that working in California would give him was beckoning.

He didn't want to lead Lois down the garden path and have her think a relationship was on the cards—but, hell, her eyes told him she wanted him and her kisses confirmed it.

They were both consenting adults, weren't they?

'I'm going to be living in California,' he told her.

'I know.'

She seemed okay with it. She knew he wasn't promising anything. But if this was going to go any further, it wasn't going to be in this tiny dressing room.

'I have a suite here.'

Her cheeks were flushed, her lips swollen, her breathing deep, making the jewels which nestled on her breasts sparkle in the light as they rose and fell.

Moment of truth.

'Stay with me tonight,' he said.

The tiniest nod of her head. 'Okay.'

It was no more than a whisper, but it was enough.

Max lifted the suitcase. This wasn't the way he'd expected the evening to end, but even if she changed her mind right now it had already been an evening which had far outshone his expectations. She'd turned up, for one thing, and outperformed every other act on the stage. And he'd held her in his arms, kissed her lips, seen desire in her stunning eyes.

But she lived in London, belonged at St Martin's and he would be leaving the first moment he could. That was non-negotiable.

'Shall I take your bags sir?' asked a uniformed porter in the foyer. 'The Royal Suite, isn't it?'

'It is,' replied Max. 'But we're fine, thank you.'

'Very well,' said the porter. 'Goodnight, sir… madam.'

Lois smiled at him.

Did he know where they were going? What they were about to do? Dear Lord, what had happened to her? The Lois she knew didn't do things like this. The Lois she knew and saw in the mirror every morning didn't have a one-night stand in one of the world's most exclusive hotels with one of the world's most eligible bachelors.

Had the world shifted on its axis?

The lift pinged its arrival and the door slid open. 'After you.'

Max nodded towards the shiny mirrored interior of the lift. Those eyes… He couldn't begin to know what they were capable of. Or maybe he did. Maybe he did this sort of thing all the time. She was probably just one in a long line.

He pushed the button for the Royal Suite. 'Are you sure about this, Lois?'

She swallowed. *Was she?*

Somehow her legs had carried her this far, and although logical Lois had put forward a reasonable counter-argument, this Lois, whoever she was, still found herself in a lift, about to go into this man's bedroom.

The lift pinged, and the sudden awareness that her heart was beating rapidly against her ribs was a warning to stop and think.

The Lois she knew was back.

The lift doors slid open. The Royal Suite was the only suite on this floor, and its large mahogany door was mere feet away, looming before her.

It was only a few steps to its threshold.

A boundary.

Her heart rate shot up further.

Logical Lois didn't want to be seduced by Max Templeton's handsome face, athlete's body and persuasive kisses. Logical Lois most definitely didn't want a relationship.

But he wasn't offering a relationship, was he? He was in London for three more months and he'd just made sure she was aware of that fact.

He held the door open for her to go first, dark indigo eyes sultry, watchful.

Could he read her mind? Could he tell she was

struggling with this? Torn between desire, fear and logic?

'I can't offer anything long term, Lois. I don't do relationships and I'm going to be living over five thousand miles away.'

'I know.' She tried to keep her voice light—not show that she didn't do this sort of thing all the time—but knew she probably didn't sound convincing. 'I understand.'

Logical Lois knew exactly what he was saying.

But she was under a spell.

And this wasn't logical Lois's night.

This night was for Lois the opera singer—the woman who'd had flowers hurled onto the stage for her, the woman who'd been cheered and told she had an amazing voice, who'd shaken hands with film stars. It belonged to the woman who'd seen the desire in Max's eyes and been kissed by him in a way she'd never known a kiss could be.

'That's fine by me.'

And there it was again. Undiluted desire flared in his eyes and she knew it was mirrored in her own.

Heart pounding, she walked to the door.

The last boundary.

He unlocked it, slotted the key card into place and soft wall lighting illuminated the hall. Kicking his shoes off and taking her hand, he led her down the corridor and into the lounge. A huge wall of windows revealed an expanse of the London city skyline, twinkling with lights from the towering buildings and the glittering river several floors below. But she didn't have time to drink it in because Max wasn't hanging around to look at it.

Standing before her, he lifted his hand to her cheek, his fingers once more softly trailing a line down her jawline to her chin, lifting it upwards, making her lips part and her eyes close in readiness as every one of her rational objections disappeared, erased by his touch.

'Lois…'

His voice was a light whisper, but heavy with desire. When his lips brushed hers their touch was soft and light, but then he pulled her to him, erasing any remaining distance between them, strong arms holding her. When he deepened his kiss she moaned, responding, raking her fingers through his hair, bringing him impossibly closer. She reached inside his dinner jacket, easing it from his shoulders, throwing it onto a nearby armchair. Her fingers were hungry to explore the shape of his broad shoulders, the strength in the muscles of his back, the warmth of his skin through his shirt.

He took his kisses to her throat and she arched her neck, drawing him down further, and as his lips found her collarbone he brought his fingers to her bare shoulders, then lower, tracing a line around her necklace and then curving over her breasts, sending fizzing darts of desire to the very place right between her thighs that ached for him the most.

His fingers found the zip at the back of her dress and he undid it. The heavy velvet fell from her shoulders and with a soft thud landed on the carpet, encircling her feet. He stopped kissing her only to stand and look at her, naked before him in the almost darkness except for a strapless bra and knickers and the gold, glittery heels. He groaned.

'You look sensational.'

The Lois she knew so well would have tried to cover herself—would have laughed off the compliment and, despite the only twinklings of light coming from the windows of distant buildings, would have been horrified that he was fully dressed while she stood almost naked before him.

But tonight's Lois was different. Tonight's Lois wanted Max. She knew the risks and was willing to take them. She'd deal with tomorrow when it came.

'Is there a bedroom?' she asked.

His eyes didn't leave hers as he took her hand. 'This way.'

She didn't notice that the bed was a four-poster... didn't notice the opulence of the fabric it was draped in or the richness of its colours, or the softness of the deep carpet. There was only Max, kissing her, crushing her to him, his hard erection pressed against her.

Her fingers found the buttons of his shirt and she began to undo them, not wanting even that fine fabric between them. Max wanted it there even less than she did, and ripped the shirt open himself, sending buttons in all directions. In another moment he'd unclasped her bra, and that champagne fizzing coursed through her as he cupped her breasts and dipped his head, running his tongue over one taut, peaked nipple and lightly squeezing the other, sending hot waves of pleasure to her very core.

He moaned as she undid the button on his trousers and unzipped him. His black satin boxers couldn't hide his huge erection and Lois knew her eyes had widened. He lifted her with ease and instinctively she wrapped her legs around his waist, gasping as his erection nudged her exactly where she wanted it to be.

Carrying her, kissing her neck, her breasts crushed against him, he laid her down on the plush bedding. She didn't want to wait another moment for him to be inside her. But he paused, reaching for his trousers, finding his wallet and a condom, tearing it open and rolling it on in one swift, practised movement. Then he was over her, his hard, toned body about to bear down.

'Max…'

It was as soft as a breath but loaded with impatient longing. His mouth met hers as he lowered himself towards her, not pausing, sinking into the wetness between her thighs, pushing into her, making her gasp and groan all at once.

Wrapping her thighs around him, she wanted to draw him deeper, but he knew what she wanted and he drove himself into her, finding the exact part of her that was screaming to be satisfied. He was all that existed. Nothing else mattered. She knew only the ever-swelling wave of desire endlessly cresting as he thrust into her with hungry greed.

She called out, almost surprised, when he brought her to the sweet, desperate edge of ecstasy, before sending her crashing over into the oblivion of orgasm only a moment before claiming his own pleasure with a final thrust, arching back, eyes closed, burying himself in her completely.

Neither of them spoke until their ragged breathing had begun to settle.

'Perfect,' he whispered, still breathless, lying on his back beside her.

'Mmm…' Her eyes were still closed. She was still savouring the sensations washing over her. Her body was relaxed, weightless, all tension gone, her skin tingling. The decision this new for-one-night-only version of Lois had made was a good one. If this wasn't right, what was?

Max rolled onto his side to face her and lifted himself on one elbow.

'It was a little fast and furious.'

Lois opened her eyes. He bit his lip in mock contrition, eyes twinkling mischievously. Dear Lord, he was handsome.

She smiled. 'Maybe a little.'

'I couldn't resist you a moment longer. We'll take it slower next time.'

He traced a finger lightly across her shoulder and down her arm, making her shiver.

He looked concerned. 'Are you chilly?'

'No, I'm okay.'

Next time?

Max stood to pull the bedding down, giving her a glorious view of his toned, strong, tanned, heavenly body.

'Get under the covers, stay warm.'

The for-one-night-only Lois who'd materialised this evening would have real Lois's gratitude for ever. Real Lois would never have been able to agree to this—would never have been able to stand almost naked before him, even in the dark. But she would always have wondered what she'd missed.

A large, gleaming copper bathtub sat at the foot of the bed. Max nodded towards it, a dark eyebrow raised. 'Seems a shame not to use it.'

And he wanted her out from under the covers.

He ran the water, tipping bath foam into the steam which rose from it, letting the bath fill as he lit the candles in hurricane jars on the table, giving the room a soft, warm glow.

Returning to the bath, he turned off the taps, swishing his hand around in the water.

'Coming in?'

Reaching for a throw, she wrapped it around herself before sliding out of bed. He took her hand as she stepped into the bath and cast the throw aside, lowering herself into the water.

Max stepped in and sat at the opposite end.

This hadn't been in the plan. Go in, get the job done and get out of Dodge asap. That had been the plan. No delays. No distractions. But he hadn't factored in meeting Lois.

He took a breath. The plan still held. He couldn't stay. He'd explained that to Lois earlier and she'd seemed okay with it. She wouldn't be here with him now if she wasn't, would she?

Lois lay with her eyes closed, her head resting on

one of the towels draped over the edge of the bath behind her. The water was warm…the vanilla scent like fresh-baked cookies. She looked completely relaxed, her breaths long and slow, her lips curved slightly upwards in a tranquil smile. The steam had settled onto her skin in tiny beads, some of which had run downwards over her neck and breasts and found their way back to the water. She still wore the emerald necklace; it rose and fell hypnotically.

The room was silent.

London would still be busy, even at this time of night, but for now they were the only people in the city. Alone, legs casually entwined beneath the warm water, peaceful, sharing this moment.

Inhaling a long breath, filling his lungs with the warm, steamy, cookie dough scent, he rested his head back and closed his eyes. It would have to end, but right now it was bliss.

'I could fall asleep lying here,' said Lois dreamily.

Max opened one eye, his stomach clenching again at the sight of her. She was so beautiful. And so damn sexy. Her breasts slowly rose and fell with her breathing, almost but not quite revealing the deep pink of her nipples through the bubbles. Clearly he'd had long enough to recover from their 'fast and furious' encounter on the bed— his reaction demonstrated that he was more than ready again.

'But that's probably not a wise move.' She opened her eyes, meeting his, and smiled. 'Can you pass me the soap?'

Max reached for the bar of soap in the dish beside him, dipped it into the water and created a lather in his hands. 'Allow me.'

Lois sat upright and held out her arm, which he took, soaping it before taking her other arm and doing the same. Kneeling before her, he soaped his hands again, and she lifted her chin as he caressed her throat and shoulders, spreading his fingers to encase her breasts, thumbs skimming over the taut nipples, hearing her gasp as he did so. She got to her knees, her waist clear of the water, and rivulets were running down her curves as she rose to allow his fingers to roam over her. She gasped again as they found a different spot from the one he'd found earlier, but one that was equally sensitive, judging by the way she arched towards him.

'Do that again,' she murmured, her eyes meeting his, full of unabashed, wanton desire.

He didn't need telling twice. And she *was* telling him, instructing him, almost daring him not to do as she demanded.

Letting his fingers be guided by the shape of her, he slipped them further down until they nudged her where he knew she ached for them. She gripped his shoulders and he felt her nails as he slipped inside her with his fingers. When they'd had sex earlier it had been the fast, frantic sex of two people who couldn't get close enough, fast enough, and although he'd felt her climax, he hadn't savoured it as he was going to savour it now. This time he wanted to give her the time she deserved. They had all night, and he wanted to draw out every sensual moment.

For it could only happen once.

Dipping his head, he took one of her nipples between his lips. She placed her hand on his head, keeping him there, but he wanted something else too. He lifted the plug from the bath to allow the water to drain away.

'I don't want this to end, Max.'

He lifted his head, taking her chin between finger and thumb, tilting her face to him. 'It's not ending yet, Lois.'

Her mouth was on his, her kiss sweet, luxurious, demanding. This woman was unbelievable. The Lois he knew from the ITU was a capable, knowledgeable professional. The Lois he'd seen on stage tonight had an amazing talent and could hold an audience rapt. But the Lois here, now, in this bedroom, was a glorious goddess—and he didn't know how long he could wait to be inside her again.

But wait he would. Because he wanted to give this woman so much pleasure. He lowered himself, crouching on his knees. The water had drained away, leaving vanilla-scented bubbles at the bottom of the glowing, candlelit copper bath. He wanted to taste her, and when he did she moaned softly, raking her fingers through his hair, arching to meet him.

And he knew he had her. She said his name just before he took her over the edge, and he slipped his fingers inside her again to feel her pulse onto them, squeezing them as wave after wave of pleasure overtook her. He rose up to take her in his arms and she almost collapsed into them, pressing her lips to his.

He reached behind her for a towel, opened it and wrapped it around her.

'Let's go to bed,' he growled.

Lois lay on the bed, her breathing still heavy, watching Max as he gave himself a rough towelling down before joining her. Her eyes, despite herself, were drawn to his huge erection, which did nothing to help ease her rapid breathing or slow her heart rate.

She met his gaze. He was grinning.

'I did say it wasn't going to end just yet.'

But as he reached for the wallet he'd dropped onto the bedside table, his face dropped.

'I don't have another condom.'

'The famous Lothario that is Max Templeton only carries one condom around with him? You do surprise me.'

Trying to supress her grin was impossible.

He sat down on the edge of the bed. 'It's not like that, Lois. That's just the papers. Do you have one...?'

'No, sorry.'

'Damn it.'

'I'm sure you could get the concierge to procure some for you. A place like this will do whatever its top clients require, I imagine.'

He turned around to face her, the agony of his disappointment apparent in his eyes.

'I'm on the pill.'

She smiled as his expression changed to one of relief, quickly followed by the narrowing of his eyes.

'You big tease.'

She laughed, dodging as he poked her playfully in the ribs.

'The concierge!' he said, poking her a second time as she laughed all the more.

'I'm sure he's very discreet,' she replied, biting her lip, trying to stifle her amusement.

But suddenly, he looked serious.

'You're definitely on the pill?'

'Have been since my teens…dysmenorrhea…so yes, definitely.'

His face softened.

His eyes darkened.

Her breathing deepened.

Dear Lord, one look from him and she was putty in his hands.

He climbed onto the bed and her thighs parted instinctively as he knelt between them.

'You're so beautiful, Lois.'

She reached for him, pulling him down towards her. He'd satisfied her in a way she hadn't known she could be satisfied, but there was still an ache deep inside her which only he could quell.

Those hypnotic blue eyes…eyes she'd seen so many times before, but never quite like this, never filled with desire as they were now…were looking at her with such longing. She knew what his eyes were capable of. She'd seen others practically fall at his feet, say yes to things they hadn't really wanted to say yes to, stare at him awestruck, enchanted by their power.

But this was something else. He was looking at her as though she was the only woman in the world...as though she was the one he desired above all others...as though she was *everything*.

And then he took her...slowly, gently. Almost too gently. She wanted him badly, right now. But he'd promised her slow, hadn't he? And he was clearly going to keep his promise.

Time stopped as he eased into her and she didn't breathe, feeling every inch of him as he entered, oh, so slowly. But soon he filled her, and when he did he stopped, pulsing gently inside her, holding his breath for a moment, his eyes closed. Then he opened them and looked at her, holding her gaze as he began to move, building the pace, building the tension within her once more, increasing her need for him with every stroke until she shattered around him and called out, gripping him with her thighs and her hands as he found his own climax, thrusting into her, growling her name, closing his eyes tightly.

Breathing heavily, he lay beside her. Still flooded with powerful, shocking, perfect waves of pleasure, she didn't want to move. If this really was for one night only, she'd remember it for the rest of her life.

CHAPTER NINE

FOR A MOMENT Lois didn't know where she was. She lay looking up at an unfamiliar ornate white plaster ceiling rose and the crystal chandelier which hung from it. She was naked and alone.

Where was Max?

The room was silent. He was probably in the bathroom. Was he coming back to make love to her again?

She closed her eyes, remembering last night—the way he'd looked at her, touched her, kissed her, sent her to the edge of places she'd never been to before and on to the sweet, powerful ecstasy beyond.

She wasn't cold, but a shiver ran up her spine. That other Lois had appeared from nowhere, conjured up by his persuasive eyes, taking control, doing things that normal, regular Lois would never have dreamt of doing. She'd been naked before him, had bathed with him, allowed him to explore every inch of her. The dim, soft candlelight had empowered her, but even so, normal Lois would have been way out of her comfort zone.

Sitting up, she looked round. The door to the en suite bathroom was open. He wasn't in there.

Reaching for the towel, she got up and wrapped it around herself. It was still a little damp from last night.

Last night... Dear Lord.

'Max?'

She padded into the lounge, the deep carpet soft and luxurious underfoot. It was as they'd left it last night, but now mid-morning summer sunlight streamed through the huge windows and the Thames twinkled far below, busy with boats of all kinds.

She glanced around. Her dress lay on the floor, a heap of green crumpled velvet. Drawing the towel around herself tightly, she went out into the hall. Her case stood by the door but there was no sign of Max.

She walked back to the lounge and sank down into one of the armchairs, grabbing a cushion and hugging it to herself. Max had warned her he wasn't staying in London for long, and that had obviously been his way of saying he was offering a once-in-a-lifetime deal.

One night of passion.

For one night only.

He could at least have waited until she'd woken up, though…couldn't he?

A sudden loud buzzing at the door made her jump. She sat upright, putting the cushion to one side. Was it Max?

'Hello?' she called through the door.

'Breakfast, madam?'

Breakfast?

Clutching the towel tightly, she opened the door an inch to see a uniformed porter with a silver trolley laden with an array of dome-covered silver dishes.

'Would you like me to set it out in the dining room, madam?'

'Oh…erm…no, thank you.'

She was practically naked.

'I can manage, thanks.'

'Very well, madam, if you're sure. Oh, Mr Templeton requested fresh juice but didn't specify which kind, so Chef has sent up a selection.'

'Thank you.'

'Good day, madam. If you require anything else, you can call me directly on the iPad in the lounge.'

Max had ordered breakfast?

Perhaps that was his parting gift? His way of saying thank you and goodbye? Was that his usual MO?

She lifted the lids on some of the dishes: sliced fresh fruits, croissants, toast… And there was a pot of tea…and one cup and saucer.

One.

For a wild moment she'd thought he might have ordered breakfast for them both. But he'd ordered it for *her*.

Thanks, Max, but I'm not hungry.

Sinking back down into the armchair, she tucked her knees up in front of her, hugging them. Had he regretted last night so much that he'd had to get away so soon? She buried her face in her hands. Oh, God, how was she going to face him at work? She groaned.

Would anybody notice if she never turned up for work again? If she took a flight to South America and never came back? If she just hid here in this hotel suite for the rest of her life?

He'd seen her naked.

She hugged her knees more tightly and buried her face on top of them.

What had she done?

She'd never be able to walk back onto her unit again. Or at least not until Max had gone off to his new life in California and the coast was clear. She had a couple of days off work now, and was grateful that was how her shifts had fallen. Maybe her blushes would have subsided a little by then.

Work.

Was that where he was? Had he been called in to see Luke?

She sat up suddenly hopeful.

But why hadn't he said so?

He could have woken her and she could have gone in too. Was Luke okay? Had something happened overnight?

She located her handbag, which she vaguely remembered dropping to the floor when Max had been unzipping her dress. Rachel, the ward clerk, answered her call, and assured her that Luke was stable.

And Max hadn't been in.

He'd called earlier and spoken to his registrar for an update on all his patients, and then he had reminded them that he was on a day off and wouldn't be in until tomorrow unless he was needed.

Her heart sank. So there was no reason he'd

needed to leave so early. No reason apart from the fact that he'd wanted to get out of there…away from her. Heat spread across her cheeks and the tiny light of hope she'd clung to was snuffed out.

So what was she supposed to do now?

Sliding under the duvet and staying there sounded like a good option.

How stupid was she?

To think that someone like Max would actually be interested in someone like her. What planet was she on? Men like him could have anyone they wanted, any time they wanted them—and she'd proved that last night, hadn't she?

There was no doubt he'd wanted her. She'd seen the desire in his eyes, felt it in his touch, his fingers, his lips. Heat rose through her, spreading, washing over her, making her skin burn and her insides flutter. It had been more than amazing. It had been unforgettable. One night only—but heavens, she'd remember it for ever.

She'd wanted it as much as he had. She'd known what she was getting into. Her eyes had been wide open. But now, despite the sunshine outside, the cold, harsh light of day had dawned and the reality of her foolishness faced her.

Had she held some naïve notion that he perhaps *liked* her? That maybe he would want to see her again other than at work?

No, of course not. That would have been silly.

So why did she feel so empty? So small? So worthless?

'Stop it,' she said aloud, sitting up straight. 'Stop feeling sorry for yourself.'

Throwing the cushion she'd been clasping aside, she stood and headed for the bathroom, letting her towel fall to the marble floor and standing under the huge rainfall shower as warm water cascaded over her.

This sort of thing happened all the time. There were one-night stands happening every night of the week. People gave themselves to each other on a purely physical and superficial basis as if it was going out of fashion—and if they all allowed embarrassment and humiliation to bother them, no one would ever achieve anything.

Reaching for the shampoo—a high-end brand she would never buy herself—she squeezed a generous amount into her palm, massaging it in vigorously. She was in the Royal suite of one of the most luxurious and expensive hotels in London, so why not make the most of it? Enjoy the breakfast Max had so generously sent as his *Thanks, but no thanks* parting gift. Lie on the four-poster bed and watch a good film, then tap the iPad to summon her personal porter to take her case and order her a taxi home.

Then all she had to do was figure out a way to work with Max Templeton for the next few weeks whilst simultaneously trying not to think about him at all.

It had been two long days since the show...since he'd seen her...since they'd spent the night together.

The best night of his life—which had been followed by one of the most difficult mornings.

Meeting the health secretary in Parliament to discuss the screening programme's progress had been straightforward enough. Going to visit his mother hadn't. If he'd ever thought she'd already hurt him all she could, he'd been wrong.

'*The famous screening programme?*' she'd sneered, lighting a cigarette. '*You've been talking about that for years and nothing has happened yet.*'

'*It's a rigorous process,*' he'd replied. '*There's the medical research, the public health viability tests, the development of IT support systems, the training of staff... Not to mention the hoops the health ministers make you jump through. But it's about to get off the ground. I thought you'd be pleased.*'

'*Hmm...*' She'd blown smoke from the side of her mouth as she'd looked down her nose at him. '*It's not going to help us, though, is it?*'

'*It'll help other families.*'

'*Too late for William, though. Much like you were when you should have—*'

She'd stopped mid-sentence, but he'd known how it ended. He'd heard it before.

'*The best thing you can do is make sure you don't have any children of your own—you'll pass the gene on and ruin another family.*'

Years and years of hard work, dismissed by her with a disdainful look and a few scornful words. Had he really expected her to find some solace in what his work had achieved? In the fact that he might help to prevent other sudden young cardiac deaths? He'd hoped rather than expected, perhaps. But it had been a vain hope, obviously.

Going back to the hotel to see if Lois was still there had also been a vain hope. She'd checked out by the time he'd done everything he'd needed to do and gone back. He didn't have her number and had no clue where she lived. Besides, seeing his mother had set every atom in his body on edge.

Why did she have to throw every single thing he did back at him?

Because he'd not done the right thing when it had really mattered. He'd cost her dearly. Because of him she'd lost her son, her husband and the life she'd expected to have.

And she'd blamed him.

And stopped loving him.

And she'd been right to.

He'd let William down. He'd killed his own father and he'd ruined her life. And his twelve-year-old self had realised very quickly that it didn't matter how many times or how hard he tried to win her love back. He had to get used to it. It was the new normal.

The only way he'd been able to deal with the new, cold, distant mother he had, had been to become the same as her. Close down. Shut his feelings away in a box in his head and padlock it. He'd thought he'd done that pretty well, but she still had the power to turn him into the twelve-year-old boy who'd seen

his twin brother lying dead on the grass and been
frozen with fear. The same boy who'd wept every
night for too long, hoping that someone would tell
him everything was going to be okay and that no
one blamed him.

He approached the nurses' station. 'Morning.'

Everyone looked up and greeted him. Lois remained seemingly engrossed in the computer screen.

She was annoyed with him.

Not unsurprisingly. His meeting with the health
secretary in Westminster had completely slipped
his mind. He'd only remembered when he'd woken
up the following morning, watched Lois sleeping
beside him and recalled the events of the night before. Remembering how she'd looked on stage had
led him to remembering why they'd been there—
to raise funds for the screening programme. And
that had led to him remembering his appointment
with the Right Honourable Mark Wallingham at
nine a.m.

He hadn't had the heart to wake her, so had decided to leave her sleeping.

That was what he should have done, wasn't it?

The right thing by not disturbing her?

Or had he taken the cowardly way out? Sneak-
ing away at dawn so as not to have to face the difficult questions of the morning after. Not to have
to risk seeing any possibility that she might feel
anything emotional. He'd honed that skill to such
a high level it was almost second nature.

Suddenly she was looking at him, emerald eyes challenging him to maintain his composure.

'I think we can discharge Luke Evans this morning. His white cell count is back to normal, obs are stable. If you can change his IV antibiotics to oral, I'll see if there's a bed on the ward.'

He needed to speak to her...explain.

'Shall we go and have a look at him?'

'Daisy will go with you.' She returned to the screen.

Daisy looked up. 'Sure. Ready now, Max?'

Lois really was annoyed with him.

'Yep, let's go. Sister, could I have a word with you afterwards?'

She stood up and straightened her uniform. 'I'm sorry, Max, I have a meeting.'

'Later, then?'

'You have a full day's clinic today,' she replied, glancing at him far too briefly.

He did. A long clinic. And an evening clinic he was doing to help with the long waiting lists. He wouldn't be done until way after her shift had finished.

She didn't want to speak to him...obviously. Perhaps it was for the best. When had he ever chased a woman the morning after? Never. So why the hell was he doing it now?

'I'd actually better get going,' he said. 'The first patients will be arriving as we speak.'

'Luke won't take you very long,' she replied over her shoulder as she stood up. 'He's much better.'

And she was gone, clutching a folder to her.

What had happened between them two nights ago had been a one-off. Possibly it should never have happened at all. But she was mad as hell with him and he needed to explain. What had happened wasn't going to happen again, but he owed her an explanation nevertheless.

CHAPTER TEN

'CAN I ASK a quick question, Max?' said Tom.

'Of course.'

He was glad of the distraction. It had been a week since *that* night. A week to think about little else other than how amazing Lois had felt in his arms… how he'd made love to her and felt like the luckiest man alive…how he wanted to see that look in her eyes once more. The look she'd had as he'd kissed her, glittering with desire.

She'd barely looked at him at all since, and when she had it had been with a cool distance. It shouldn't have bothered him. But it did. Which concerned him.

'Alfie Martin,' said Tom. 'CVP has been teetering all day. It's down at two. BP ninety over forty. I think he's a bit dry.'

'Sounds it. I'll come and have a listen to his chest—just to make sure he's not overloaded and fluid's sitting in the wrong places. I don't want to risk any pressure on his graft.'

'Some help at bed four, please!'

Lois's tone told him the patient she was with took priority.

He strode over, threw back the curtain, glanced at the monitor, saw the figures and clocked the patient's deathly pallor.

Lois was turning up the IV fluid via the central line.

'Jay Vallini's patient: aortic arch aneurysm repair this morning, stable all day, but he's just dropped his BP and gone very tachy. Could be a leak.'

Max addressed Tom, who'd followed him over. 'Call the lab to bring up two units of blood. Asap.'

This was bad. The familiar dread filled him. This man's life was literally flowing out of him, and if he didn't act swiftly the patient was going to bleed out before their eyes. He checked himself. He knew what he was doing. He'd done it many times. This patient would receive the best of him—he'd do everything he could not to let him down.

And try and do that without snapping at the staff for once.

'I'll get the ultrasound.'

Lois still didn't look at him. She'd remained coolly professional all week. He should be grateful. He didn't want to get involved, and her reaction to what had happened between them told him that she didn't either. Perhaps it was her way of dealing with a one-night stand.

And he'd thought *he* was the master of *love-'em-and-leave-'em...*

'Need any help?' asked Daisy, peering in.

'No,' replied Max.

Daisy stood aside, allowing Lois to come back in with the scanner. Max reached for the trolley just as Lois pushed it alongside the bed. Their fingers touched and they both looked up at the same moment, their gazes clashing, something passing between them.

Something that pulled him in.

It was only a moment, but it was enough for him to know that he wanted more.

Before he knew it Lois was back in professional mode, as though nothing had happened. They'd connected again…and lost it. It had been only a second, but it had made him feel more alive than he had in a week.

'Substantial bleeding,' said Max, moving the probe, studying the image on the screen. 'He'll need to go back to Theatre.'

'I'll call CT,' said Lois, turning to leave.

'No time,' replied Max. 'The ultrasound has said enough.'

Tom appeared, holding two units of blood. 'Check it with me?'

Lois reached for a giving set and switched on the blood warmer.

'Get that in stat,' said Max. 'I'll ring Theatres.' He glanced through the patient's notes on the iPad, waiting for someone in Theatres to pick up. 'Ed? Hi—Max Templeton. I need to bring a patient to Theatre asap. Sixty-four-year-old chap; George Frost; aortic arch aneurysm repair from this morning. He's got a significant leak, so we'll need to open him up again. I'll be there in five and I'll be bringing the patient with me.'

But the response from Theatres wasn't what he wanted or expected to hear.

'There must be *someone*.' He glanced over to Lois and Tom, who were both staring at him, concerned. 'We'll be there in five minutes. Prep the theatre, get me a bypass machine and tell the staff I'll bring my own scrub nurse and anaesthetist.'

Lois stared at him. 'Problem?'

'The theatre staff are tied up with multiple patients from an RTC. Orthopaedics have taken up two theatres. We can use an empty theatre, but in terms of staff there's the on-call perfusionist and they can only spare a couple of runners.'

A frown creased her forehead. 'But you told them to get the theatre ready and that you'd get your own staff.'

'Toby will anaesthetise,' replied Max. 'I know he's not doing anything this evening. And you have theatre experience.'

Her mouth dropped.

'Lois, I know it's a big ask, but if we don't do this, we'll lose the patient.'

And he wasn't about to do that. He lost patients—of course he did. All surgeons did sometimes. It was never easy. Most surgeons dealt with it by reminding themselves that they'd done their best and could have done nothing more. But Max wasn't most surgeons. And to him, losing a patient was a personal blow—one he tried to avoid at all costs.

He turned to Tom. 'Your chap in bed three… I've got three minutes. Let's go.'

Lois glanced up as he left and the coolness of her gaze stung him. But he only had himself to blame for that. He'd set out the rules.

No promises.

There was no point in regretting that now.

It was what they both wanted.

Their time together had been limited to one amazing night.

It was meant to have been enough.

But it wasn't.

Gloved hands steepled in front of her, Lois stood at the theatre table, waiting. Toby was at the head of the table, dealing with the ventilator, monitoring the patient's vital signs and administering the blood which was just about keeping the patient from crashing. Deepa, the perfusionist, was checking the heart-lung bypass machine. The runners stood poised, ready to carry out whatever was asked of them during the surgery.

Max, who was once again pushing boundaries, strode in. She'd managed to avoid him pretty successfully for the last week, but now she was going to have to stand only a few inches from him for at least a few hours. But then it would be over and she could go back to pretending he didn't exist.

He took his place on the opposite side of the table. His scent was too familiar, and way too intoxicating, and her unruly heart began to thud hard in her chest.

Damn him for doing that to her.

'Ready?'

He glanced at Toby, who nodded.

'Bypass okay?'

Deepa gave a thumbs-up.

'Sister?'

His eyes met hers and heat rose within her as

they took her back to their night in the Savoy—to the last time she'd been this close to him.

'Ready.'

Pretending he didn't exist hadn't worked all week, if she was honest with herself, and it certainly wasn't working now.

'Scalpel.'

She placed a blade firmly into his outstretched palm.

'Music.'

Soothing classical music filled the room and Lois glanced around at everyone's bent heads. All of them were concentrating on the job at hand, Toby humming lightly. She placed the suction tubing, giving Max clear sight into the opened thorax. He held out his hand and she handed him retractors, clamps, artery forceps and cannulas without him having to ask.

'Ready for bypass in five. ACT okay?'

'ACT is fine,' replied Toby. 'But BP is in his boots and sats are down. He's lost a lot of circulating volume.'

'Cannulating,' said Max, taking the lines from Lois, who held them out ready.

Watching him, keeping careful track of the progress he was making, she ensured she was ready to pass the correct instrument at exactly the right moment. Every second counted—this patient was in a bad way. It was mesmerising, watching Max at work. His hands moved deftly and with precision. Even though he was under enormous pressure.

'Dividing the lines.'

He hadn't looked up since the surgery had begun. Head bent, moving swiftly, calling out instructions, he worked on his patient. A patient who, if Max hadn't been around when he had, and reacted as quickly as he had, and if he hadn't made a highly irregular request of her, might no longer be with them. It was still touch and go, but at least Max's actions were giving him a chance.

'Off and clamped,' said Deepa.

'Aorta connected,' he replied. 'Line test good?'

'Good swing and pressure,' said Deepa.

'Cannulating atrium…return losses,' replied Max. 'Ready for bypass?'

'All good.'

'On bypass,' said Max.

And then he looked up, meeting her gaze, making her heart kick against her ribs. He had one moment while the perfusionist made her checks. And he'd chosen to spend it looking at her. Dark-lashed, deep blue, his penetrating eyes looked up from over his mask, the weight of immense responsibility visible in them. The soft classical music still played and the ventilator clicked as Toby paused it. Monitors beeped. It was her and him. And despite the fact that he'd walked out on her, leaving her hurt and humiliated, she didn't want it to end.

'Bypass is good,' confirmed Deepa, breaking the spell.

And Max was gone. Back to his work. She could breathe again.

Max Templeton had cast some sort of spell over her, and if she had the time to think about it—which she didn't right now—she'd know he'd just made her want him now as much as she'd wanted him all along. And that was exactly what she'd wanted to avoid.

Jay Vallini appeared in the doorway. 'Want me to scrub, chief?'

Max didn't look up. 'I wouldn't mind. He's lost a lot of blood, and the aortic arch is so friable it's difficult to find anywhere suitable to graft.'

'I'm not too surprised it's leaked,' replied Jay, disappearing to the scrub room. 'His vessel disease is very advanced.'

'There's just no viable tissue,' replied Max.

Lois glanced at him. There was a hint of tightness in his voice.

'Pressures aren't great, guys,' said Toby, glancing up at them. 'Blood markers are showing AKI.'

'One hour on bypass,' said Deepa.

The pressure on Max was huge. This patient was deteriorating, and it didn't look as though they were heading in the right direction.

'It's not looking great, Max,' said Jay, now standing beside him and inspecting the patient's open thorax. 'There's nowhere else to graft.'

Max didn't look up. 'I'll find somewhere.'

'He lost most of his circulating volume before you got to him, Max,' said Toby. 'It was a pretty massive bleed. I'm not sure he's going to make it.'

Max said nothing. But Lois saw, beneath his mask, that his jaw had clenched.

'His sats aren't improving, even on bypass,' said

Toby, 'and I'm giving him whole blood and packed red cells. I think we're losing.'

Max sucked in a deep breath, his mask drawn inwards as he did so. 'I just need to get the graft in place. Stay with me.'

Was he talking to the team or to the patient?

Suddenly the chest cavity filled with blood.

'Damn it,' said Max. 'Clamp.'

Lois passed him a clamp, then used the suction to try to clear the area so he could see.

This was bad.

'Cannula's gone,' said Jay.

Toby looked up. 'Sats dropping.'

'Clamp is on,' replied Max.

The bleeding stopped.

'Jay, you recannulate. I'll do the graft.'

Jay Vallini sighed. 'I think it's over, Max.'

But Max ignored him. 'I'm going to put the graft here. Cannula in, Jay?'

'In,' replied the older surgeon.

But he glanced at Lois, his eyes telling her he thought this was pointless. Her head told her he was probably right, but her heart told her to cling on to the same hope Max clearly had.

She glanced at him. His jaw was set, the tendons in his neck tight.

'Sats?' he demanded.

'Improving,' replied Toby.

'Good,' said Max.

For another hour they worked on the patient and steadily his vital signs improved, remaining stable when they took him off bypass.

Lois saw the change in Max. His shoulders relaxed and his jaw unclenched. He really cared, didn't he?

'I'll close up and get him to ITU, chief,' said Jay. 'You get home; you deserve it.'

'I'll just write up the op notes,' replied Max, moving away from the operating table and snapping off his gloves.

'Do that if you must,' replied Jay. 'But then you're officially off duty—I insist. I'm covering.'

'Thanks, Jay,' said Max.

Lois caught his eye as he left the theatre, squashing any thought that he might have looked at her on purpose for some reason.

No, he'd made his feelings very clear, hadn't he?

She was good for one night.

Nothing more.

Not even good enough for breakfast the next morning.

But she'd agreed to his terms and conditions, hadn't she? She'd been warned. And she only had herself to blame for how she was feeling now.

'Suture, please, Lois.'

She forced a smile as she handed Jay Vallini a suture. She still wanted Max Templeton—and it hurt like hell that he didn't want her back.

Theatre was quiet. The machines lay silent and redundant. The music had stopped. The lights were off.

Max was still writing up the op notes in the adjoining office and he'd probably be a while. From what Lois had seen, his notes were precise and exceptionally thorough. He might be the playboy the media described him as, but she couldn't deny that he really cared about his patients.

Finally off duty, Lois had gone to get changed when she'd realised that she'd left her pager on the table in Theatre. Now, dodging back into the darkened room, she picked it up.

She sensed Max before she turned around. It was as though the air suddenly contained electrified particles of him which reached her and, on touching her skin, ignited, making it tingle.

He stood in the doorway, an imposing, impressive silhouette, backlit by the light from the scrub room. Her breath caught in her throat and she stopped dead in her tracks.

'At last.'

He walked slowly towards her into the darkness, panther-like. Lois took a step backwards as he advanced.

'I've been trying to talk to you for days. You've been avoiding me.'

'Hardly.' She took another step backwards, bumping into the theatre table where they'd been standing earlier that evening. 'I've seen you nearly every day.'

'Yet you've still managed to make yourself scarce.'

She gripped the black padded table behind her to steady herself. 'I should get back.'

'You're off shift. I need to speak to you.'

Her heart hammered in her chest. She didn't want to speak to him.

Did she?

'I wanted to say I'm sorry.'

'There's nothing to say sorry for.'

There was quite a list.

'For not being there the other morning.'

'No need.'

It was better he hadn't been there. It would only have been awkward. He clearly regretted their night together.

'I'd forgotten I had an early meeting in Westminster that morning. I couldn't miss it and—'

'You could have woken me.'

What? Where had that come from?

She was glad he'd slunk off and ended their ill-judged tryst.

But he'd had a meeting.

He hadn't slunk off because he'd wanted to.

'You looked so peaceful. I didn't have the heart.'

She glanced around sharply. 'Shh…someone might hear.'

'There's no one down here…and I've locked the door.'

'What?'

'You've been darting out of my way any time I've come anywhere near you. I had to do something.'

He looked at her, and she couldn't think of anything but how she wanted to be lost in his eyes, his arms.

He'd had a meeting. He hadn't slunk away be-

*cause he hadn't wanted to face her. She didn't need
to feel humiliated. He hadn't meant to hurt her.*

'Why didn't you tell me?'

'I told you: I'd forgotten about the meeting and
only remembered when I woke—'

'No,' she cut in. 'Why didn't you tell me afterwards?'

'I tried. You were avoiding me. I couldn't get
near you. And every time I tried you apparently
had to be at some meeting or other, or anywhere
else I wasn't.'

'Have you heard of telephones?'

He sighed. 'I don't have your number—and before you say anything, I couldn't very well ask any
of the staff for it, could I? How would that have
looked?'

She lifted her chin. He was probably right. It
would have looked odd to ask for her mobile number.

'Email?'

'Email?' He repeated the word as though it was
the most ridiculous thing he'd ever heard. *'For the
attention of Sister Newington. Apologies I was ab-
sent from bed the morning after we slept together,
but I had an appointment with the health minister
which had completely slipped my mind. See you on
the ward round.'* He folded his arms, resting his
chin on his fist. 'Hmm… I'm not sure that's great
hospital email etiquette.'

'Oh, all right—point taken. But you could have
tried harder. I don't remember you trying to speak
to me particularly.'

He spread his arms wide. 'Lois, I've tried everything. I sat down beside you at lunch the other day and you leapt up, telling me your break time was over. I waited for you after the Gold Command meeting, but apparently you had to rush off. I even went to the chapel to see if you were doing your choir practice.'

Lois rolled her eyes. 'Well, I won't ever be doing that again—it got me into all kinds of trouble.'

'Lois…'

He took a step towards her and she gripped the theatre table more tightly. His warm, musky scent filled her nostrils and she was immediately transported back a week, to the opulence of the Savoy and the very nearly perfect night they'd spent together—marred only because he'd disappeared the next morning, leaving her wondering why.

'I'm sorry I didn't try harder, but I've finally tracked you down now and I want to apologise. I couldn't get out of the meeting but I wish I could have stayed. Maybe I should have woken you, but I didn't have the heart. I thought about leaving a note, but I didn't have time—and anyway, I'd intended to be back before you checked out. But you'd gone by the time I got there.'

'I stayed for hours! I had breakfast…watched a film. You hardly *rushed* back.'

He sighed. 'I had a lot to do that morning and it took longer than I'd expected. I'm sorry. I know how it must have looked.'

'It looked like you regretted it.' She met his gaze, determined not to fall under the spell of his eyes.

He swallowed, appearing to struggle to decide which words to speak, and when he did they were spoken with conviction, even though they were only a whisper.

'Far from it. Every moment of that night is etched in my memory.'

Her heart slammed into her ribs.

Did he really mean that?

'I'm not here for long, Lois, but while I *am* here I'd like to spend some time getting to know you. If you don't want to then just say, but I haven't been able to stop thinking about you since that night.'

Same here.

Her mind was whirling. She didn't want a relationship. She'd fought her instincts when Emilio had been making his advances. Not hard enough, as it turned out.

And why had that been?

Because, stupidly, she'd believed his lies. Emilio had appeared, fed her a few compliments and she'd decided to rebel against everything her mother had ever told her. And it had ended in her complete humiliation. Emilio had used her. Was she about to make the same mistake with Max?

But Max was looking at her with those *Take me now* eyes, bewitching her, enticing her to believe his words…

He lifted his hand, touching her chin, lifting it between thumb and forefinger. Heat flooded through her as she looked into his eyes…shooting through her and settling between her thighs, exactly where he'd touched her that night and sent waves of pleasure coursing through her.

She didn't want this.

But she did.

He held her gaze and her resolve weakened.

His voice was low and husky. 'I missed you that morning.'

Dared she believe him? If she did, would she find out too late that it was a lie?

'I wanted to wake up with you and make love with you again, with the sunshine streaming in through the windows.'

Then it was better that he *had* gone before she woke up—because he would have been disappointed. The only way she'd been able to get naked with him that night had been because she'd known the only light had come from a few flickering candles. The summer sunshine streaming in through the enormous windows in the morning would have been a complete dealbreaker.

'Well, you had a meeting, so…'

Tilting her chin, she took a breath, trying to ignore how his warm scent and the nearness of him gave her butterflies, which wouldn't listen to her when she silently begged them to stop dancing in her stomach.

This was Emilio all over again, and she wasn't falling for it.

'So that's why I'm here…that's why I've been trying to track you down for days and speak to you…why I've had to resort to locking the door to a theatre.'

'I can't actually believe you've done that. Isn't that entrapment, or something?'

He took a step back, his brow suddenly furrowed, and she immediately missed his proximity. Slipping his hand into his pocket, he produced a silver door key, offering it to her.

She looked down at it. She could easily take it from him, unlock the door and leave. She didn't want another T-shirt with *Lois is a gullible idiot* printed on it.

So why wasn't she reaching for the key?

Because, in spite of what she kept trying to tell herself, he wasn't like Emilio, was he? He *hadn't* used her. He'd given her plenty of opportunities to walk away that night—just as he was doing now. But she hadn't wanted to and she didn't want to now.

Besides, he wasn't exactly committing to spending the rest of his life with her, was he? This was a no-risk, once-in-a-lifetime chance to enjoy life, have some fun. No promises, no expectations, no danger of a broken heart. She was just creating some exciting memories to look back on one day. And proving her mother and Emilio wrong. She *was* attractive.

The *other* Lois was back. The risk-taking, daring, you-only-live-once Lois from the night of the show.

The very same Lois who'd slept with Max a week ago.

And had the night of her life.

'You've driven me crazy all week, Lois.' He was

still standing back from her...cautious...watching. 'I needed to explain and I couldn't get near you.'

She searched his eyes for tell-tale signs that he was lying...and didn't see any. He took a step closer and she gripped the table, her nails digging into the thick black rubber.

'That day in the staff restaurant, when you ran off as soon as you saw me approaching...even though you'd left half your coffee behind... I so nearly came after you.'

She dropped her gaze so that she could take a breath.

He took a step.

There was only a breath of air between them now.

And that was too much.

'Lois?'

She looked up into piercing blue eyes and was instantly lost...immediately transported back to the hotel suite, when she'd stood before him and he'd slipped her velvet gown from her shoulders. Her skin prickled with fizzling champagne bubbles.

He paused, his eyes seeking and clearly finding her acquiescence.

And then he kissed her.

After the micro second it took her to return his kiss, he deepened it, then traced a line of kisses to her throat. This felt as right now as it had in the hotel over a week ago. And the reason she'd thought about little else since was right there, in his kiss. Heat blazed through her and her skin burned for his touch. Reaching up, she wove her arms around his neck, drawing him closer. He groaned and whispered her name as he lifted his head from her throat, trailing soft kisses back up her neck before his focus returned to her lips, now warm, swollen, and desperately wanting to taste more of him.

'Are you sure the door is locked?' she murmured.

'I wouldn't do *this* if I wasn't sure…raise your arms.'

And, taking the hem of her scrub top, he lifted it up, pulling it over her shoulders and head, letting it drop onto the table behind her.

He took a long breath as he looked at her, raw desire flaring in his eyes, orange flames blazing within the dark blue pools.

'You are so unbelievably gorgeous.'

And she felt it.

Hooking his fingers under the straps of her bra, he pulled them down before reaching around her back, unclasping it. The weight of the release of her breasts into his warm hands as he cupped them, his thumbs skimming her nipples as they peaked at his touch made her gasp.

'Max…'

His hands held her waist, his fingers slipping under the waistband of her scrub trousers, pushing them down until they fell around her ankles and she could step out of them. She pulled at his top, reaching up, her hands running the length of his hard, toned torso as she did so. He grasped it, taking it from her when she could reach no further, tearing it off over his head and throwing it behind her onto the table.

When he lifted her, she instinctively wrapped her legs around his waist, gasping as the hard evidence of his arousal nudged her. The theatre scrubs did nothing to restrain his desire, and the ache deep within her only intensified as, dipping his head, he took one nipple and brushed it agonisingly lightly with his tongue, making her arch backwards, face upturned to the ceiling. Her body pushed into his, wanting only to be closer. He turned his attention to the other nipple, and the sweet agony at the loss of his mouth on her was only momentary as he sucked. Her hand went to his head, fingers raking through his dark hair, bringing him closer, urging him on, needing more.

Pushing her knickers to one side, he skimmed his thumb over her, taking her breath. Her arms around his neck, she adjusted her position so that she was over him, in exactly the place she wanted to be. The need to have him inside her was almost more than was bearable.

'Hold on tight,' he whispered.

Her eyes widened and she held on around his neck, her thighs gripping his waist. Suddenly she remembered their motorbike ride dash across London, when he'd given her the same instruction.

'Because we're not going for a Sunday drive?' she said.

He grinned: a wide, sexy-as-hell smile which lit up his flaming blue eyes with an erotic wickedness.

'No, it's not going to be a Sunday drive, Lois.'

Letting go of her with one hand, he pushed his

scrubs down before grasping her thighs again firmly.

'You sure?'

His voice was dark, throaty, heavy, his eyes brim-full of desire. His erection was poised—tantalising torture, ready for her agreement—and his ripped chest was expanding and falling with his heavy breathing, the muscled contours catching the dim light coming from the next room, making her want to touch them.

But she needed to hold on.

'I'm sure.'

The words left her lips, but barely had a chance to escape into the crackling air around them. Because no sooner had she said them than his lips were on hers, crushing them, silencing her and the soft moan that followed.

'Hold on,' he whispered again, his eyes glinting.

She held his gaze as he thrust inside her with a groan, closing her eyes only a moment after he closed his own as hot desire flooded through her. Then, exquisitely, he held still, just for a moment, allowing them to savour the feeling...the sweet bliss and the agony of wanting more all rolled into one. And then he began to move...slowly...his eyes locked onto hers.

As she arched back, taking him deeper, the look on his face in the dimly lit room, told her she'd just intensified his pleasure too, and he picked up the pace, his breathing deepening, his skin glistening with a sheen of sweat. The strong muscles of his chest and arms were taut, moving rhythmically like a beautiful machine, sending wave after relentless wave of pleasure flooding through her, filling her; warming her. He was sending her closer and closer to the edge with every stroke as he drove into her, building the sweet pleasure-pain tension deep inside her until she groaned his name, letting her head fall back as he took a nipple into his mouth.

She shattered around him, eyes squeezed shut, whispering his name. 'Max…'

'Don't let go.'

'No,' she managed. 'I won't.'

He slowed his rhythm, as if he wanted to savour his release a moment longer, but she knew the moment he allowed it as a deep, guttural groan left his lips. His head went back as he thrust one last time, and the light hit the curves of his chest as he arched, beaded and glistening with sweat, his breathing fast and ragged until he lost control over its rate and surrendered to the all-encompassing moment of oblivion.

She let out a satisfied sigh. She'd made a choice tonight. She was choosing to live a little.

And it felt amazing.

CHAPTER ELEVEN

LOIS FOUND HIM in the chapel, sitting at the back, elbows on his knees, head in his hands.

She sat down on the bench beside him. 'You did everything you could, Max.'

He sat up, placing his own hand over hers where she'd rested it on his thigh. 'Obviously not everything. His daughter was devastated.'

'Everyone else had given up on him. You gave him a chance and an extra week of life he wouldn't have had. Don't beat yourself up.'

He withdrew his hand. 'I should have got that graft in more quickly.'

'Max, stop it. He was desperately ill. Even Jay Vallini said he'd been in two minds whether to operate in the first place. It's really sad, but you gave him a chance—it just didn't work out.'

'Because of me.' He stood, clearly wanting to leave.

'Where are you going?'

'Home.'

'Do you want me to come with you?'

She remained sitting, looking up at him, into those indigo eyes which couldn't hide his anguish. He cared deeply about his patients, and it had become more and more obvious the longer she spent with him. He tried to hide it, for some reason, and most people might not have noticed the little give-away signs that revealed just how much his patients meant to him.

The way he touched their hand, arm or shoulder when he spoke to them…how he'd sit with relatives answering questions until they had no questions left…how he came in early to check every patient each morning and stayed late doing the same before going home, even after a busy clinic or theatre list.

'No.'

'But I put a chilli in the slow cooker this morning and you said you'd be my guinea pig and try it.'

He looked down at her and she gave him her best puppy dog eyes, complete with turned down mouth.

'You promised.'

He shouldn't be on his own tonight. Not when he was feeling the way he clearly was. In the last week they'd spent almost every evening together, either at his flat or hers, and tonight it was her turn to cook.

A soft, gentle smile curved his lips. 'I did promise that, come to think of it.'

Returning his smile, she stood. 'Come on, then.'

He still looked forlorn. Her instinct was to take him into her arms, but they'd both agreed to keep whatever it was that was happening between them outside working hours—well away from the all-seeing gossipmongers of the hospital and hidden from any potential press interest.

Anyway, she had the rest of the evening to try to lift his mood.

Lois had the most comfortable sofa he'd ever sat on. It was as large as a bed, strewn with brightly coloured throws and huge cushions, and you sank down into it as if it was a giant marshmallow. It would easily sleep a family of four.

He set the wine glasses and what remained of the bottle of wine they'd had with dinner on the coffee table. Lois lit the candles in the jars she had dotted about the room, then sank down beside him. Draping his arm around her shoulder, she nestled into him, sipping her wine.

This felt comfortable...right. He kissed the top of her head and she looked up, a soft smile on her lips. But he tensed when he saw she wore the same look she'd worn in the chapel earlier.

A look of concern.

For him.

And he didn't want to see that...not in anyone's eyes and especially not in hers.

'Do you want to talk?' asked Lois.

'Not really.'

Not at all. Because that would involve bringing up subjects he really didn't want to talk about, wouldn't it? And if she knew the truth she might reject him, as everyone else had done.

For some reason, it was more important than anything that she didn't do that.

'Actually, forget that,' she said. 'We *need* to talk.'

'We do?'

'Your patient. George Frost.'

'Oh.'

Damn it.

'You struggle with it, don't you?'

'With what?'

'Losing a patient?'

His breathing deepened.

Don't go there, Lois.

'A little.'

Not the fullest answer he'd ever given to a question, but it was more than he'd ever given anyone else.

'Because of what happened to your brother?'

He stiffened.

Too close to the truth.

'Probably.'

She sat up straight, his arm falling from her shoulders as she turned to face him. He watched the dancing flame from one of the candles, not wanting to see any hint of kindness in her eyes. Tiny wisps of dark smoke drifted up from the wick, swirling upwards before disappearing. He drained his wine glass.

'That wasn't your fault either.'

His stomach clenched. In his head he knew that as a twelve-year-old he couldn't have been expected to resuscitate his brother...not really. But his head wasn't in charge of how he felt. It had been *his* fault. He hadn't done anything to help when William had collapsed. He'd not only let William down—he'd ruined their family.

Afterwards, the family had never been the same again. His mother had barely been able to bring herself to look at him. His father had found comfort at the bottom of a bottle, and Max struggled to remember ever seeing him completely sober ever again. He'd died almost a year to the day after William. And Max's world had imploded for a second time.

If he told Lois all that—if he could even find the words to do so—she'd never look at him in the same way again, would she? She'd feel sorry for him...pity him. And he didn't want that. Which meant he really didn't want this conversation.

'I guess losing William just means that I don't want to lose anybody else, and that's why I find it difficult to lose a patient. Grief is hard, isn't it? I don't want to put anyone through that if I can help it. So, yes, I have a tendency to morph into a bit of a raging bull if I think one of my patients might die and, yes, I'll do anything to save them. I'm well aware that people around me sometimes think I'm an arrogant braggart at those times.'

'No-o-o!' said Lois, grinning. 'I've never heard anyone say that.'

He laughed. 'I'm sure you have.'

Lois pretended to think hard. 'No, not arrogant braggart... Maybe a pompous prat, or an egomaniac, or...'

'Okay, okay, you can stop. I get the gist.'

At least he'd managed to change the subject.

'Tell me about William.'

He stiffened and drew in a breath.

Maybe he hadn't.

But he could tell her a little.

'We were twins...best mates...did everything together. We were as thick as thieves most of the time, but we could argue and scrap like we'd been trained for it at others. We were close.'

'I'd have loved a brother or sister.'

'I only had him for twelve years.' He picked up his phone and scrolled, stopping at a photograph and holding it to show her. 'This is us.'

She glanced at him before looking at the photo and gasped when she saw it. 'You're exactly the same as each other! What a lovely photo.'

He managed a thin smile. 'That was taken a week before he died.'

A week before his world imploded.

She sighed and looked into his eyes. 'I'm so sorry, Max. I can't begin to imagine how hard that must have been. Were you there when it happened?'

He swallowed. 'We were in the garden, playing football. He just collapsed. He was running around one minute and gone the next…snuffed out like a candle…in a second.'

She closed her eyes for a long moment, opening them again and looking at him with such pity he could barely look back at her.

'Your parents must have been devastated. Their only comfort would have been in still having you.'

The bitter laugh left his lips before he realised. 'Not really, no.'

But he didn't want to give her the whole story—the complete account of how he'd let his brother and his family down and how his parents had never forgiven him. What if she felt the same? What if she blamed him too?

'My father died a year later, and I was shipped off to boarding school soon after. My mother barely spoke to me after that—other than to remind me never to have children myself.'

'But you don't have it, do you...the valve condition?'

'No. I was checked out almost straight away after William died. My echo was normal. But of course there's a genetic risk. I'd never have children...no way. I'd never want to put another family through that.'

'I see... I can't imagine what you all went through. It's awful your father died, and so sad your mother reacted in that way. Have you tried to build a relationship with her as an adult?'

He sighed. 'A few times. There's only so much rejection a person can take, though. I've given up trying now. It's too late.'

'Perhaps, because you look so alike, rather than seeing you as a comfort she was reminded of William and it hurt too much. Still, it's terrible she reacted that way.'

'In truth, it's one of the reasons I'm leaving for California. Living in the same city, I feel obliged to go and see her. But every time I do, I get told the same thing and I'm reminded that she'd prefer William to be there than me. I can't keep doing that—and quite honestly the sooner I leave this place, the better. Anyway, enough of this... I sound like I'm looking for pity—which I'm absolutely not. Drink?'

He wanted to end this conversation. Lois was

too kind, and spilling everything out to her would be way too easy.

'Please,' she replied, shifting a little so he could reach the wine bottle.

'Let's change the subject,' he said.

She held her glass out and he took it and topped it up.

'Any news on the screening programme?'

He relaxed. 'Going to plan. The NHS trusts in the pilot have received their funding and are completely on board. The first scans will begin at the end of the month. Which reminds me—how do you fancy a weekend in Monte Carlo?'

'Seriously?' She took the glass from him.

He grinned. 'I've been asked to go and visit a patient I operated on six months ago. He was a Hollywood heartthrob in his day. He gave me a very handsome donation for the programme and he's on holiday in Monte Carlo…on his yacht, of course. He's wondering if I'd pop over to review him…all expenses paid.'

'You're kidding?'

He took a sip of wine. 'No, not kidding. And I want you to come with me.'

'When? I'll have to see when I'm on shift.'

He smiled. 'Lois, you're the only person in the entire world who, when offered an all-expenses-paid trip to stay on a luxury superyacht in Monte Carlo, would say she has to check her shifts first.'

She raised an eyebrow and grinned at him. 'Well, I do… So your wealthy Hollywood patient will have to wait until I'm free.'

Drawing her legs up onto the sofa, she nestled into his side as he planted a kiss on top of her head. He'd escaped the inquisition about what had happened with William...for now. But if they continued to get closer, as they had been, it would surely come up again, and he was pretty sure that Lois wouldn't let him get away with avoiding the topic a second time.

CHAPTER TWELVE

ANCHORED JUST OFFSHORE, the yacht had a top deck that was a perfect vantage point to take in the stunning alpine vista. Belle Epoque and art deco architecture mingled with ultra-modern skyscrapers tapering towards the shoreline, nestling below a backdrop of rugged mountains. The harbour was crowded with watercraft: enormous cruise liners, yachts of all sizes, brightly coloured bobbing boats and RIBs. The sunlight on the blue of the Mediterranean made it shimmer with almost blinding brightness.

Lois marvelled at the view. Max lay beside her on a sun lounger, eyes closed, shades covering them, naked apart from swimming shorts, and glistening with the sun lotion she'd just more than enjoyed applying to his perfect body.

'Are you ogling me, Sister Newington?' he asked, without opening his eyes.

'Just checking I haven't missed a bit.'

She *had* been ogling him. Watching him and wondering how on earth she'd ended up here, being wined and dined by one of Hollywood's finest actors, on a superyacht, in one of the most exclusive resorts in the world.

And besides all that she got to sleep with the gorgeous man who lay beside her, looking like a Greek god who'd just competed at Olympia.

If her mother could see her now...

'It won't last. He's just using you for what he can get and you're giving it to him. Men want women they can show off in front of their friends, boast about, imagine other men being jealous over. They don't want a plump plain Jane.'

She could almost hear her mother's voice, scornful, disapproving, contemptuous. But her mother wasn't here, was she?

Max sat up slowly and removed his shades. 'So it's okay if I check you out too, is it…? Just to make sure you haven't missed anywhere with your sunscreen?'

He grinned, and Lois pulled her sarong around her. She'd braved wearing a swimsuit—before they'd jetted off she had scouted round the shops to buy one that promised to hold her in all the right places, also finding a couple of matching sarongs for an extra layer of security.

'I was just going to get a drink,' she replied. 'Do you want one?'

'I want *you*,' said Max, standing, striding over, and straddling her lounger before planting a kiss on her lips. 'I'm not sure how I'm managing to keep my hands off you…lying there semi-naked, looking like a dream.'

She took his face in her hands, pulled him to her and kissed him back. 'Well, you'll have to try—because we're not exactly alone here, are we?'

The yacht had more staff than guests—which of course had its advantages, but meant that someone might appear offering food or drink at any moment.

'I'll save you for later, then. Fancy a swim?'

Her heart sank. The prospect of walking across the deck in front of Max in nothing but a swimsuit, even if it was one that promised to hold everything in, filled her with dread. He'd seen her naked many times in the last few weeks, since they'd embarked on their very secret affair, but only ever in lighting that had been low enough for her to feel comfortable. The bright morning sunshine of this glorious Mediterranean summer's day gave her nowhere to hide.

'I think I'll just stay here. You go.'

'Come on, it'll be nice. And besides...' He grinned and slipped the edge of her sarong from her shoulder. 'I want to see you properly in that sexy crimson swimsuit.'

Every part of her screamed *No!* and she shifted her position, pulling the sarong back into place. 'It's not sexy...it's just a swimsuit.'

'Everything on you is sexy. A bath towel...a onesie...your uniform.' He drew in an exaggerated breath and pretended to shiver. 'No one else wears that uniform like you do.'

'When are you going into the clinic to give Art his check-up?'

'Why are you changing the subject?'

'I've just remembered you're here to give Art his check-up, that's all.'

'After lunch. He's taking us to the casino this evening, as a thank-you. If I go for a dip, will you slather me in sunscreen again afterwards?'

'My pleasure,' she replied, picking up her book again. 'Enjoy.'

She watched over the top of her book as Max strode towards the pool. It was like watching an advert for male swimwear—except that she wasn't looking at a TV, he was right there in front of her. Bronzed, lean and beautifully muscled. He sat on the edge of the pool and dropped down into the blue water, his head disappearing before surfacing again, dark hair wet and blacker than ever.

'It's lovely, Lois. Come and dangle your feet if you don't fancy a swim.'

It was tempting.

And it wasn't.

'Maybe… I might just finish my chapter.'

He gave a thumbs-up and struck out, making his way across the pool with long strokes. The pool sparkled in the sunlight as his arms sliced through the water, scattering glittering crystals back onto the surface. It did look inviting.

Would the crimson swimsuit do everything the persuasive sales assistant had promised? Hold her in? Smooth her out?

There was only one way to find out. Anyway, Max had told her so often now how much he loved her figure she was almost beginning to believe it. *Almost.*

Clutching the sarong around her, she stood and walked quickly over to the pool, but a wave of nausea washed over her and she sat down on the side, closing her eyes until the accompanying dizziness passed. The midday heat here was something else.

Max smiled up at her and stood, smoothing his

hair back from his forehead as he rose out of the water, skin glistening.

'You okay?' he asked, frowning. 'You look a bit pale.'

'I'm fine. I stood up a bit quickly, that's all. It's the heat.'

'Are you coming in? It'll cool you off.'

'I'm okay here, thanks. I'll watch.'

'Okay. Kiss me first.'

Lois pretended to look horrified, and pulled back as he moved in for a kiss. 'No, you're all wet.'

He grinned a mischievous, sexy grin, and she laughed as he moved closer, standing between her knees. He took her by the waist, pulling her towards him, planting a kiss on her oh, so ready for him lips.

She looked down at her costume. 'You've made me all wet.'

He looked down too, and bit his lip in mock contrition. 'Oh, dear. You may as well come in, then.'

She laughed. 'You're incorrigible.'

'I think you might have said that to me before.'

'It must be true, then.' She prodded him playfully on the shoulder, but he still had hold of her waist and she shrieked when he lifted her. 'Put me down!'

'You said it.'

He let go of her and she splashed down into the chest-deep water, letting out another shriek, her sarong floating up behind her.

'You…!'

'Now, now, Lois, let's not have any bad language on board this very posh yacht.'

Sweeping her hand through the water and up-wards, she sent a cascade of glittering water over him, making him cover his face. Laughing, she did it again. But he responded in kind and drenched her. The sarong was soaking wet. There was absolutely no point in keeping it on.

Apart from the fact that it covered her *'voluptuous'* figure.

Mutton dressed as lamb.

No.

Stop.

They were words from the past. She didn't need to hear those words right now. Right now, she wanted this moment.

'God, you look gorgeous.'

He'd stopped scooping water and now stood a few feet away. An Adonis—just looking at her. No, not just looking. *Admiring.* The look in his eyes was one of admiration.

Butterflies.

Dancing butterflies.

Twirling, looping, fluttering.

There was no reason not to believe him. Shrugging the sarong from her shoulders, she let it fall into the water, her eyes not leaving his as she did so, watching him as he drew in a breath, pausing before moving through the water towards her and taking her in his arms. Drawing her in to him, he kissed the top of her head.

'You look so good I could devour you.'

She allowed him to pull her into his arms. Was

she making the same mistakes she had with Emilio? Was the same old deep-seated need to be validated by someone else still lurking like a predator below the surface, ready to pounce? Even though she'd tried so hard to unmask it, understand it and over-come it?

He let go of her and stood back, looking into her eyes again, a frown creasing his forehead and con-cern etched on his face.

'You didn't hug me back. What's wrong?'

'Nothing. Go and enjoy your swim. I might get out and read a little more.'

'I don't want you to get out and read. I want to know why you suddenly changed.'

'I'm just not that keen on swimming, that's all.'

'Or on receiving compliments…especially about how you look?'

She stared back at him. He'd mentioned compli-ments before…that night after the show. But he'd never been specific about the sort of compliments she struggled with the most. He was right, though.

'Where does that come from, Lois?'

Her heart rate notched up. 'From looking in the mirror.'

She laughed. If she made light of it maybe he would too.

But his frown only deepened. 'Why would you say that?'

'Well, I'm not exactly a supermodel, Max, am I?' She forced a laugh. *Keep it light.*

'Thank goodness. You're amazing as you are.'

'Voluptuous?'

She smiled, but could see immediately that Max wasn't convinced by it.

'That was a compliment,' he said.

'Well, *"voluptuous"* sounds much better than fat.'

Why could she suddenly feel the sting of tears? She turned away from him and began to wade towards the edge of the pool, but he reached for her arm and she was forced to turn back to look at him.

Deep blue eyes looked into her own. 'You're not fat.'

'No, I much prefer voluptuous—that's what I've called myself ever since you said it.'

Don't cry, Lois.

She tilted her chin. 'So, thanks for that.'

But somehow trying to smile again only brought her closer to tears.

His frown returned. 'Somebody has hurt you, Lois. Who? Tell me.'

His eyes searched hers…beautiful, earnest blue eyes, lulling her in as always.

Did she want to tell him?

She swallowed, staring down at her hands, swishing them on the surface of the water. For some reason she wanted to explain to him. It was because his eyes told her that he cared about her answer.

'She didn't mean it.'

'Who didn't?'

'My mother.'

'What?'

'I understand why…now. It took me a long time, but I realised that she just did it to keep me by her side…because she needed me.'

'What did she do?'

'I was her carer when I was growing up, and she was quite needy. I did everything for her—she never left the house.' Lois reached for her sarong, scooping it from the water, needing to hold on to something. 'She'd tell me I wasn't pretty…that I was overweight…and that no one would ever want me… But it's fine. I know why she did it. I'm fine with it now.'

Max stood with his hands on his head. His mouth had fallen open. 'Well, that explains a few things. Why didn't you say anything before?'

'Why would I? And what do you mean, it explains a few things?'

'You're uncomfortable whenever anyone compliments you—like you can't believe it. You're so capable and confident at work, and yet you can suddenly close down. Sometimes I only have to look at you a certain way, or tell you that you look beautiful, and your whole demeanour changes. Oh, Lois, I hate it that you went through that. I wish I could change it.'

'You have, Max. You've definitely helped. It's just a slower process than I'd imagined, that's all. But I'd never have worn this until I met you, for starters.'

She spread her arms wide, giving him her best *Ta-da!* pose.

He smiled. 'If I said you looked amazing, would you believe me?'

She drew in a breath. *Would she?* There was nothing but honesty in his face.

'No, don't answer that. It was unfair to put you on the spot like that. Hear this instead: Lois, you look amazing in that swimsuit. Stunning, gorgeous and sexy as hell. So, come here and give me that hug.'

She waded through the water towards him, a smile spreading slowly across her face as she watched his eyes darken in that way they did…the way he looked at her when he wanted her. He took her into his arms and she wound her own around him, pulling him closer, leaving him in no doubt that she was hugging him.

He dipped his head, nuzzling into her neck. 'You don't know what you do to me, Lois.'

But she did. She could feel it through the crimson fabric.

CHAPTER THIRTEEN

'SHALL WE WALK up to the clinic rather than get the car?' asked Max as they alighted from the tender in the harbour. 'We should make the most of this gorgeous weather. It'll probably be raining back in London.'

The heat was so intense that she'd have been glad of a car, really, but Max was right. In another few days they'd be back in London. She was glad of the wide-brimmed straw hat the woman at the swim-wear shop had somehow persuaded her to buy, and she pulled it low to shield her eyes as they wound their way up through narrow streets towards the clinic for Art's check-up.

Stopping beside a low wall, with a stunning view down the cliffside and out to sea, Max stood behind Lois, his arms around her waist. 'Beautiful, isn't it?'

She was glad he was holding on to her. Was it the heat or the height that was making her feel light-headed? Maybe they should get a car back…

'Gorgeous.'

He released his hold of her. 'I want a picture of you… Turn around so I have both you and the view.'

And that was when everything went black.

In a haze, Lois felt the squeeze of a BP cuff on her arm and the light pressure of a sats probe on her finger.

Where was she?

'BP's up to a hundred over sixty,' came an unfamiliar voice with a French accent.

'I need an ECG.'

Max's voice…steady but laced with concern. He was clearly addressing someone else. Unfamiliar fingers lifted her top and placed stickers on her chest. Her head felt heavy and nausea swept through her.

Unfamiliar faces swam into view. She must have fainted.

It would be the heat.

'Sharp scratch on your arm, Lois.'

A different voice. A blood sample.

This was all very unnecessary.

She'd just overheated, and was perhaps a little dehydrated. She tried to sit up, but suddenly Max came into view and he gently pressed her down.

'Lie down, Lois. You fainted, and we're just trying to find out why. You'll be fine, but stay lying down until your BP comes back up.'

'ECG, Doctor.'

One of the nurses handed him a sheet of print-out paper.

Lois watched his face as he read it, the concern vanishing as he looked at her and smiled. 'It's fine. A little tachy, as expected, but otherwise normal.'

'BP one ten over seventy.'

'Feel as though you can sit up a little?' asked Max.

'Yes, please. I don't like being a patient.'

He held out his arm and she took it, pulling herself forward as one of the nurses levered the back-rest out.

Max handed her a glass of water. 'Drink this—you're probably a bit dehydrated. I'm going to call Art and postpone his appointment until tomorrow—you need to rest.'

'There's no need to do that. I'm fine now.'

But Max had taken his phone out of his pocket and was already tapping the screen. 'I'm calling him and I'm going to get the car to take us back. Don't argue.'

She sipped at the cold water, embarrassed by the fuss, her inbuilt loathing of being the centre of attention compelling her to want to run. But Max was clearly not letting her go anywhere until he was satisfied that she was okay.

And suddenly she realised why that felt so extraordinary. It was because it was new. No one had ever cared that much before.

Max had already changed into smart trousers and a shirt and was sitting out on the balcony of their cabin, looking across the pink-and-peach-streaked early-evening sky, thinking about earlier, when Lois had fainted, and what it had done to him.

His reaction had been instinctive, fuelled by the surge of adrenaline which had rushed through him, his mind racing, automatically fearing the worst… that she had an undiagnosed cardiac condition.

He'd carried her into the clinic, his heart banging against his ribs, where he'd barked out urgent orders to the staff, fear gripping him, his ambition to end his perceived reputation as arrogant forgotten.

It had been much more than his need to save every patient that had made him feel sick to his stomach for the few minutes it had taken him to realise her heart was fine.

Lois was much more than a patient.

Much more than a colleague.

And she'd become much more than a short-term, mutually agreed hook-up.

How on earth had that happened?

Because the most unlikely thing had happened, that was how.

He'd fallen in love.

So now what was he supposed to do? Tell her? Did he even dare to hope that she felt the same? Would it make any difference to anything if she did?

Her life was in London and his new life—his long-planned fresh start—was five thousand miles away. Only three more weeks before he left London. That had always been the plan. Get the screening programme over the line and then wheelspin out of there.

But as each day passed and his leaving date got closer his heart grew heavier.

'Can you do my zip?'

Turning to look back inside the cabin, he drew in a breath, taking her in. Wearing a black, sleeveless, knee-length cocktail dress, fitted at the waist and curving over her hips, she was elegance personified. A double string of pearls hung at her throat, drawing his eye down to where blonde curls lay on the generous curves of her breasts. His instinctive reaction didn't surprise him—he'd got used to Lois having that effect on him.

He left the balcony and walked over to her. 'You look gorgeous…far too good to waste on going to the casino… Let's stay here.'

Lois managed to dodge his kiss, laughing and pretending to look horrified. 'No, no, no. I've spent ages putting this face on—don't mess it up.'

He gave a fake groan and grinned at her. 'Here, I'd better do that zip, then.'

Running his finger down her spine, he zipped her up, planting a light kiss on her shoulder when he'd completed the task. He badly wanted to swing her round to face him and kiss her full on the lips, but she'd already slipped her heels on, picked up her clutch bag and shawl, and was heading for the door.

'Are you sure you feel well enough to go tonight?' he asked.

She grinned at him, and every promise he'd made to himself not to fall in love vanished.

'I'm fine. And anyway, according to you, I've got to lose my gambling virginity.'

'If you're sure you're okay?' he replied.

She never failed to surprise him—strong, sassy Lois.

'Here, you've forgotten your phone.' He picked her phone up from the table and handed it to her, glancing at the screen and frowning. 'You've got a missed call. It's a French number. Could be your blood test results.'

CHAPTER FOURTEEN

'I CAN CHECK it later,' said Lois. 'The driver will be waiting, and the—'

'Check it first,' Max cut in. 'Please.'

'The most it's going to show is mild dehydration.'

'Let's just make sure. They've left a voicemail—it'll only take you a minute to listen to it.'

'Okay.'

Someone being so concerned about her was definitely still alien but oddly nice at the same time. She picked it up and dialled, listened to the voicemail.

And froze.

Hands shaking, she pressed Repeat and listened again, unable to take in the words.

Tu es enceinte.

You're pregnant.

She looked down at the phone as though it was something she didn't recognise.

It didn't make sense. The test must be wrong.

But her recent nausea, the light-headedness and the faint suddenly all made sense.

The phone fell out of her hands onto the sofa, where it landed with a soft thud.

Max's words were echoing in her head…

'I'd never risk having children.'

'The sooner I leave this place the better.'

She looked up into deep blue eyes, concerned… questioning, and her hand instinctively went to her belly.

'What is it?'

She hardly knew how to say the words. Didn't know if she could.

She was pregnant.

He didn't want this.

'Lois, what did they say?'

She swallowed, confusing, conflicting thoughts swirling around in her head, none of them making any coherent sense.

He didn't want children.

She couldn't tell him.

'Lois, for God's sake. What did they say?'

'I'm pregnant.'

It was a strangled whisper. She dropped her gaze, not wanting to see the undoubted horror in his eyes.

He didn't speak, but she could hear that his breathing had deepened, feel the sudden tension in the air between them.

'You said you were on the pill.'

His voice was barely audible, but there was an unmistakable accusatory tone in his words.

'I was… I am. I… Maybe I forgot to take it once.'

Their eyes met. Lois searched for reassurance.

Take me in your arms. Tell me it's all going to be okay.

But neither of them could find words. A thick, heavy silence hung between them, palpable, like a barrier keeping them apart.

Max sat down in an armchair, his elbows on his knees, head in his hands, covering his face, muffling his words. 'This can't be happening…'

But it was.

She looked down at her hand, which lay gently, tentatively on her belly, where Max's baby lay nestled inside her…tiny, innocent…and unwanted by him.

When had it happened? Had she forgotten a pill?

She must have. This was her fault. And Max clearly thought so too.

'I'm sorry, Max. You don't have to be a part of this if you don't want to.'

He looked at her for a long moment, as though a million thoughts were flashing through his mind all at once and he was unable to make sense of any of them, as though he didn't quite recognise her.

'Maybe they're wrong.'

He relaxed slightly, as though that was the conclusion that made the most sense to him and there was still hope that this wasn't real.

But it *was* real. Her recent nausea, her reaction to the heat, the faint earlier… It all made sense. Anyway, somehow she *felt* it. There hadn't been a mistake. She was pregnant.

But Max was tapping on his phone.

'What are you doing?' she asked.

'Calling the clinic.'

'There's no mistake, Max. Think about it.'

He stopped dialling, but continued to stare down at his phone.

'I've had nausea; I fainted this morning. It all adds up. I'm pregnant.'

'You can't be.' He stood up, hands on top of his head, turning around to face the balcony, looking away from her. 'You *can't* be.'

'The casino…'

'What?' He spun round, looking at her, incredulous.

'We're meeting Art at the casino.'

'I don't think that's happening tonight—not now. Do you?'

'You should let him know.'

He sighed, shaking his head and reaching for his phone. 'I'll text him. I don't want to speak to him. I'll tell him you're still feeling unwell.'

'I'm not "unwell", Max—I'm pregnant.'

'Stop saying that.' He slammed his phone down onto the table. 'How the hell did this happen?'

'Seriously?'

'It was a rhetorical question.'

He sighed again, and paced out onto the balcony, bracing his hands on the railing and staring out to sea.

Was she supposed to feel entirely responsible for this? If he thought that, he wasn't being entirely fair.

She followed him, but stopped in the doorway before stepping outside. Suddenly there was a wall between them. He didn't turn around.

'I'm sorry, Max. You obviously don't want this. And of course you don't have to be a part of it.'

He swung around and stared at her, frowning as though she'd said something he didn't understand.

'You think I won't accept my responsibilities? If you think that, Lois, you don't know me at all.'

Perhaps it was sinking in.

'I'm just letting you know that I understand this

isn't in your plan. I don't want you to feel you have to change anything…your new job, for example.'

He laughed harshly. 'You think this changes nothing? Lois, this changes *everything*…you have no idea.'

Lois looked down at her hands, at the dark pink polish on her fingernails. Because of her job, she could rarely wear nail polish, but she'd gone to the salon and enjoyed choosing a colour for their holiday. She'd been excited about spending a week in the sunshine with Max…not knowing this was how it would end.

With him out on the balcony, a wall around him so thick that even a battering ram couldn't break it down, and her somehow unable to take the few steps that would take her to be beside him.

Suddenly, Max was a million miles away. Soon he'd be five thousand miles away for real. When he left for his new life. The life he'd worked so hard for, for so long.

'I know it does, but we can manage. You can still go to California, if that's what you want to do.'

But she didn't want him to. She wanted him to stay with her and the baby.

'I've signed a contract in LA.'

And he didn't want to stay, did he? He was telling her loudly and clearly that he didn't want her. He was rejecting her. He'd told her right from the start that he wasn't staying—that he had other, better things to do— and she'd understood.

But that had been before she'd fallen in love with

him. Before the baby. Did she expect him to change his mind now?

She wasn't enough for him to stay.

'And you can still go there.'

They were the hardest words for her to say, but she had to give him the freedom he'd yearned for…

Because she'd stupidly fallen in love with him.

'It would be a lawyer's dream if I reneged on my contract at this stage.' He turned back to face the ocean, leaning on the railing. 'Damn it.'

'You don't need to renege on it. You can still go.'

'You just don't get it, Lois.'

'Then tell me. Tell me what I don't get. Because we're being confronted with a situation which most people would find joyous, and you're turning it into some kind of disaster movie for no good reason.'

Max pressed his palms to his face and drew in a long, slow breath before he looked at her again, his eyes glittering. 'No good reason?'

His voice was low and so quiet that it sent a shiver down her spine.

'Of *course* there's good reason. What did I tell you about my having children?'

'That you didn't want them.'

'I *can't* have them,' he corrected. 'Can you remember why?'

'You don't need to speak to me as though I'm five years old, Max. Because of the genetic risk.'

'There's a tenfold increase in the chance of this baby having valve disease. *Tenfold*, Lois.'

'But there's screening now—the screening will pick it up if it's there. And it may not even be there.'

Max threw up his hands. 'Well, that's great, then! The baby will have aortic valve disease...but at least we'll know about it in advance. Cool!'

'Even if the test is positive—which it might not be—the surgery can be done before birth.'

'Again, Lois, you haven't thought this through.'

Why was he so angry?

'I understand why you have concerns, but you're overreacting. The screening programme you've worked on all these years—'

'Was never meant to be used to diagnose a child of *mine*.'

'Look, I know you've never wanted this, but the reality is that this baby is coming now; it's real. And I for one am glad you developed the screening programme, because it might just save our child's life.'

'You can't have the test until twenty weeks.'

'I know.'

'Which is...when? Well, we don't know, do we? However many weeks from now... That's weeks and weeks of worry.'

'I'm not worried.'

He stared at her as though she was mad. 'Well, you should be.'

'Why?'

'Because there's a significant risk, Lois.'

Max took a step closer, so that they were almost touching, and lowered his voice further. It was carefully controlled, like a warning.

'And if there is a valve defect? Who do you think will do the surgery I've pioneered?'

She looked up into his eyes. Eyes that had lost

the look of admiration she'd begun to grow used to seeing…eyes that now blazed with torment and anguish.

And then it hit her. 'There's only you…'

'And I can't operate on my own child.'

His voice was cold as ice and her skin prickled. She stared back at him. Into eyes that had lured her so many times. Eyes that had been so full of desire that she'd begun to believe that her mother and Emilio had been wrong. Eyes that now looked at her as though she'd let him down…in the worst possible way.

'I see.' She lowered her gaze.

'So how can I feel "joyous" about this?'

'You've trained others.'

'I'm *training* others—there's a difference. The plan is that after the trial is finished I'm going to return for a few weeks to complete any surgery that's needed, and train up Jay and a few others while I'm doing it.'

She flinched at his anger. If ever she'd day-dreamed about telling the man she loved that she was having his baby, it hadn't been this that she'd imagined as the scene that followed. Tears pricked her eyes but she swallowed them away. She was having a baby. And it looked as though she was the only one of them who felt any joy about that. She didn't want the tiny life growing inside her to somehow sense that it wasn't welcome. Max wasn't thinking clearly, and she didn't want to be around that.

'I'm going to get changed.'

Picking up her dropped phone and handbag, she walked back to the bedroom, took off her dress and sat on the bed. It was a shock to him. Hell, it was a shock to her. Perhaps, in the morning, after a good night's sleep, when the initial shock had settled, they'd be able to talk more easily.

She rested her head back onto the soft pillows, curling her legs up. There was no point in crying over spilt milk—this was happening and they both had to get used to it.

'Still ticking?' said Art Beauchamp, as Max pulled the stethoscope from his ears.

'Definitely ticking. Echocardiogram next.'

Max hadn't come to bed last night. He must have slept on the sofa in the lounge. When Lois had woken, he'd already showered and dressed and was sitting out on the balcony in the morning sunshine, reading something on his phone. When he'd realised she was walking towards him, he'd stood and announced that he was going for a swim on deck.

There had been no chance of any kind of conversation on the tender to the harbour, or in the car up to the hilltop clinic, as Art had accompanied them and chatted away about his latest film project.

Lois picked up the ultrasound gel which had been warming. 'Ready, Art?'

It was a relief to be in the cool clinic, away from the blazing heat of outside, but the atmosphere between her and Max was even cooler than the air being pumped out by the air con.

Art made a show of bracing himself as Lois squeezed gel onto his chest. 'Let me have it, Nurse.'

She smiled as he grimaced. 'Not too bad, is it?'

'It can be darn cold if it isn't warmed properly,' the actor faux-complained. 'I'm sure it can't be good for your heart, making you jump like that. So, how long have you two been an item?'

Lois glanced at Max, but he was turned away from her, concentrating on the echo images of his patient's heart.

Were they an item? If they had been, the news they'd had last night seemed to have changed things...drastically.

'I met Lois when I started my stint at the hospital in London.'

That was very diplomatic...and vague.

'Three months or so, then,' said Art. 'A long time for you, Max. You're not going to settle down on us, are you?'

What was this? Some kind of confirmed bachelors' club? Should she remind them that she was actually there?

Max removed the probe. 'Your valve is looking good.'

Nice save.

'Wonderful,' said Art. 'Wires next? And what was your lovers' tiff about?'

'Yep, an ECG next,' replied Max, wiping off the gel with a tissue and ignoring Art's last comment. 'And then we'll get some bloods sent off to the lab and you're all done.'

'Funny, isn't it?' said Art conspiratorially to Lois

as she attached the ECG leads. 'How a heart specialist has never been able to sort out his own heart. Perhaps you'll be the one to fix him.'

'Keep still, Art,' said Max. 'I need to be able to interpret the trace, and you moving around like that is making it look as though a spider has crawled all over it.'

Art grimaced at Lois. 'Someone's rattled his cage. We'll have a good night tonight, Lois, even if this one...' he nodded towards Max '...is still in a strop. What's your game? Blackjack? Roulette? Poker?'

None of the above.

'I'm a complete novice,' she told him.

Art's eyes glittered. 'Awesome. Well, don't worry. You have a couple of old timers to teach you everything we know.'

'We have to fly home this evening,' said Max, tearing the ECG paper from the machine and scrutinising it. 'Something's come up.'

Lois stared at him, then quickly remembered that Art was on the couch between them, no doubt watching her reaction.

'Oh, that explains the bad mood, then,' said Art. 'Well, you're welcome to take the Gulfstream back. Let me know what time and I'll get the pilot organised. Work, I assume? Well, it won't be long before you come to LA, my friend, and leave all this on-call business behind you. Life will be much better then.'

'Nothing untoward going on there,' said Max, placing the ECG trace on one side. 'Remnants of your previous heart attack, but nothing new. Thanks, the jet would be great, but we can easily take a commercial flight.'

'A clean bill of health, then?' said Art. 'And no, no. I won't have you flying commercial; take the jet.'

'You'll live to fight another day. Thanks—any time this evening would be good. Now bloods— just rest your arm on the side, please. Tourniquet?'

Lois handed him a tourniquet. He took it without looking at her, wrapping it around Art's arm and feeling for a vein. She handed him the tray with the syringe, needle and blood bottles.

'Thanks, Lois,' said Art pointedly, making Max look up at him.

He pressed his lips together, saying nothing.

Lois smiled at Art. He'd clearly noticed the tension between them, and for some reason he was taking her side. But when he found out—if he ever found out—that she'd just ruined his friend's life, he'd maybe change his mind.

Max pressed a cotton swab into the crook of Art's arm as he withdrew the needle. 'We should get the lab results in a day or two.'

'I appreciate it, Max.' Art stepped down from the couch. 'I'll get them to call you when the flight's arranged. Make the most of your last few hours of sunshine.'

Max busied himself labelling the blood bottles on the other side of the room and Art touched Lois's arm as he headed for the door.

'Ignore him; he'll come round. Whatever you've

rowed about, he'd be a fool to let it come between you for long. Max might be many things, Lois, but he's no fool.'

And with a wink, he was gone.

Art was right. Max was no fool. She watched him handing the labelled blood bottles to one of the clinic staff and give them instructions. This time yesterday she'd been the patient and he'd taken care of her. He'd taken great care of her. And it had been quite overwhelming. But now, less than twenty-four hours later, it was as though he couldn't bear to even look at her.

And he'd cut their holiday short. It was over.

Was he going to cut her loose too? Or was he just in shock? Perhaps Art was right there too. Maybe he'd come round.

But coming round to the idea of having a baby he most definitely didn't want was a pretty huge ask.

CHAPTER FIFTEEN

MAX NUDGED THE volume up higher, knowing it wouldn't fully obliterate any of the thoughts that were swirling through his mind at a hundred miles an hour, but hoping it might dull some of them.

Picking up the first flatpack box, and not bothering to read the instructions, he began to attempt to construct it. Lois was taking the rest of her planned leave from work, so he hadn't seen her in the few days since they'd got back from Monte Carlo. She'd sent him a text to say she was booked in at Queen's Hospital for a scan the next day at three p.m., and he was welcome to attend.

Should he go?

Probably—he had a responsibility.

Did he want to go?

Hell, no.

He wanted to turn the clock back and for all this to never have happened.

All this?

Including Lois?

None of this had been in the plan, had it?

Screening programme.

California.

New life.

That was the plan.

The packing box refused to play ball, and in frustration he threw it to one side. 'Goddammit!'

He had two weeks left before his flight left for

LA and he'd barely made a start on packing. He'd found other things to do instead. Like extra shifts at work…extra sessions at the gym; the extremely well attended leaving do the staff had arranged for him—although Lois hadn't been there. He could have had all the packing done by now if he'd put his mind to it. So what had stopped him? Was something deep in his subconscious mind telling him he didn't want to leave?

He'd almost told Lois he loved her, hadn't he? He'd not quite got so far as to allow the words that had formed on the tip of his tongue escape from his mouth, but it had been close.

And that must mean something.

He did love her.

He wanted nothing more than to be with her.

Right now.

But he'd hurt her. From twelve years old onwards, his life had been spent trying desperately to ensure that no other family's lives would be destroyed. He'd worked hard to become a cardiac surgeon, created the screening programme, developed the foetal surgical technique, saved every patient he could.

He'd done all right.

He could never have hoped to undo what had happened to William, but he'd generated something good from something so bad.

Until now.

Now, he'd messed up big-style. He'd vowed never to have children so that he wouldn't be the cause of even more pain. So that he didn't hurt anyone else.

But now he'd done just that. And the person he'd hurt was Lois...the woman he loved...the woman he should have protected...the woman whose life had been turned upside down because of him.

Queen's Hospital was unfamiliar territory...which was exactly why Lois had chosen it for her maternity care. There were the same familiar smells as in every other hospital she'd ever been in, though. Cleaning fluid, disinfectant, the faint floral scent of the air freshener being pumped out at regular intervals from the devices on the wall.

She'd been to Reception, checked in, changed into a hospital gown and now sat waiting to be called, her clothes in a plastic bag on the floor beside her.

Max hadn't shown up.

Every time the door had opened her stomach had lurched, but every time it had been someone else who'd come in—excited, happy-looking couples, fathers-to-be with a protective arm around their partners. But no Max.

She'd hoped that over time he might have moved on from the initial shock and come to terms with the fact that he was going to be a father. He'd said he wouldn't shy away from his responsibility, but that could have meant anything. Maybe he meant he'd send money—not that she wanted it. He was obviously still planning to leave to go to his new job in California—she hadn't been able to bring herself to go to his leaving do and had insisted she work the shift on the unit to allow others to go.

Doing this alone was a daunting prospect, but an exciting one too. She wanted this baby. If Max didn't, she understood why. Having a child had never featured in his life plan. He'd worked all his life towards the moment when he could leave London and begin his new life. That moment had arrived for him. And neither she nor the baby were enough to make him want to stay.

What was wrong with her that once again she'd fallen for a man who was completely emotionally unavailable? Would staying in London to be with her and the baby be such a bad thing? Not if he loved her. If he loved her, he'd change his plans—it wouldn't be a big deal.

But he didn't.

So it was.

The problem was, she'd fallen for him…and she was hurting.

She could never have believed it was possible to hurt so much.

Crushing, aching, desperate pain.

And anger.

At herself for having fallen for him.

And, illogically, at Max for making her do so.

Max strode quickly towards the radiology department. He was late, but he'd had to review a transplant patient who appeared to have developed sepsis. He'd dealt with the patient, written up the treatment plan, had him admitted and then had run to his bike, roaring across London to get to Queen's.

He knew his registrar could have dealt with the case, but as usual he'd been unable to walk away without making sure his patient was stable. Anyway, the patients helped him to focus. They took his mind off Lois. The second he wasn't with a patient Lois was there, filling his senses.

Lois.

The woman he just couldn't get out of his mind.

No matter how hard he'd tried.

She'd tempted him to want things he'd ruthlessly taught himself not to want.

Happiness. Family. Love.

Falling in love with her had been too easy.

So easy he hadn't even seen it coming.

Which meant his defences—usually titanium grade—had been down.

Completely.

The coolness between them was killing him. It seemed to have been mutually agreed without them saying anything at all to each other. It had somehow just happened.

But it was for the best.

That was what he'd repeated to himself as he'd packed and got ready for his flight…as he'd tried to fall asleep at night…as he'd found himself pulling on his helmet and revving his bike, ready to go over to her place and tell her he loved her.

But he'd turned off the engine and gone back inside.

Because, although he desperately wanted to speak the words he'd never spoken to anyone else, he couldn't face her.

Because she'd tempt him all over again.

And he'd only hurt her.

Again.

He saw the sign: *Maternity Ultrasound Department.*

He swallowed. Suddenly, his feet were glued to the floor. What was he doing here? This was something he'd never wanted. Something that had never, ever been in his grand plan. But Lois was in there. The woman he loved. Going through this…because of him.

'You going in, love?'

He turned and saw a woman in a cleaner's uniform smiling up at him.

'Come with me. I'll show you where to go. First time, is it?'

'First time…? Yes,' he replied, still rooted to the spot.

'Aw, come on…don't be nervous. They might be able to tell you if it's a girl or a boy. It's amazing what they can tell these days.'

A girl or a boy. If that was the only question that needed answering he might be able to move his feet and go and do what he should be doing— being with Lois.

The woman held the door open for him, smiling kindly. 'Have you got a preference?'

'Pardon?'

'Boy or girl?'

'Oh, no…not really.'

'As long as it's healthy,' she said. 'That's all any of us want, isn't it?'

His chest tightened. 'Yes,' he managed. 'That's all we want.'

Somehow, his feet carried him to the waiting room.

She wasn't there.

He was too late.

'Can I help you?' asked the receptionist.

'Lois Newington. Her appointment was at three... am I too late?'

'Are you Dad?' The receptionist smiled at him kindly, but his stomach lurched at her words.

Dad.

A word he'd never thought would be associated with him.

He wanted to run.

He wanted to see Lois.

'Yes...'

'She's in room four. You're not too late. Georgie! Would you take this gentleman to room four, please?'

Heart hammering, he pushed the door open.

Lois was lying on a couch in the darkened room. The sonographer was poised, with the probe ready to scan, but paused as Max entered.

'Hello?' The sonographer looked at him.

'This is Dad,' said the nurse called Georgie, who stood in the doorway just behind him. She gave him a nudge. 'You can go and sit by Mum to watch the scan.'

'Thanks,' he replied as she left.

That word again.

'Hi,' said Lois.

'Hi.'

Was this real?

He pulled a chair over and sat down, staring at the as yet blank ultrasound monitor.

What was he doing here?

'You made it, then?' said Lois.

'Yes.'

'You okay?'

A pause. 'Yes,' he replied. 'You?'

'A little excited,' she replied.

She was smiling. Her eyes were bright, her cheeks flushed. She looked beautiful...radiant.

'Ready?' said the sonographer.

'Very,' replied Lois.

Max watched as the ultrasound probe made contact with Lois's abdomen. He looked up at her face...the face he loved...watching as she smiled when she saw her baby for the first time.

And then she frowned.

She gaped, her hand flying to her mouth.

What? What was it? What had she seen?

The heart valves wouldn't be visible at this stage.

His stomach lurched and he turned sharply to the screen, realising instantly why Lois had reacted with such shock.

'Well, you two seem to have worked it out for yourselves,' said the sonographer, smiling broadly. 'You're having twins!'

Joy and anguish collided—conflicting emotions crashing into each other. Horror. Fear. Wonder. There were so many questions he couldn't answer. So much instant and terrifying fear and anger that he didn't know where to begin.

He wanted to take her in his arms.

He wanted to close his eyes, open them again and for this not to be happening.

This was all his fault. He'd known he must not have children. He been warned to let the horror that had destroyed his family die out with him. He'd been told time and time again not to pass it on.

And now that was exactly what had happened.

History would repeat itself.

His worst nightmare.

No. It was even worse than that.

He'd done this to the woman he loved. He was the direct cause of a whole new nightmare that would affect even more lives.

When would this ever stop?

'Are they okay?' asked Lois.

'Everything's looking fine so far,' replied the sonographer.

'From what you can tell at twelve weeks,' said Max.

It would be another two months for the cardiac screening. Two…long…months. Of worry. Of wishing he wasn't the cause of it.

'Of course,' replied the sonographer. 'We'll get you booked in for your next scan before you leave today. But in the meantime you can relax, because everything looks fine…with both of them. Would you like a photo?'

'Please,' said Lois.

She was beaming…joy shining out from her.

'Here you go.' The sonographer handed a black-and-white image of the twins to Lois. 'Pop back through to the changing room, and when you're ready they'll book you in for your next appointment.'

She left the room, leaving them alone.

Lois was looking at him, and he saw her joy slowly evaporate.

'They're fine, Max.'

'You can't say that, Lois. We don't know that. It'll be another two months before we know that.'

'And there's no point in worrying over it until we do know,' she replied, sitting herself up and swinging her legs over the side of the couch. 'Why spend two whole months worrying about something that might never happen?'

'Because the statistics—'

'Are just statistics,' she replied, easing herself off the couch and slipping her feet into her shoes. 'I'm not going to waste time being worried. If there's a problem it'll be picked up and dealt with—in the meantime, I'm going to enjoy being pregnant.'

Brave Lois. His brave, sassy Lois.

The temptation to take her into his arms and allow the words that were suddenly on the tip of his tongue to be said was enormous.

I love you.

They were the words he should be saying right now. They were the words Lois deserved to be hearing.

And he couldn't say them.

Because Lois deserved so much, and he wasn't the one who could provide anywhere near what he wanted for her. How could he care for her when he couldn't even care for himself? How could he give her security and protection? And as for love... The only people he'd ever loved, he'd hurt. And the latest proof of that was standing right in front of him.

What Lois and the babies would be put through because of him was something he'd have given anything to avoid. But avoiding it would have meant he'd never have got to meet her at all. And the thought of that was physically painful.

CHAPTER SIXTEEN

LOIS HAD NEVER seen anyone visibly pale the way Max had done when the twins had appeared on the screen. He'd just looked at her, his jaw tight, a vein at his temple pulsing hard. And, as much as she might have wanted him to, it had been clear he wasn't going to take her into his arms and tell her everything would be fine.

And that had hurt.

They'd gone their separate ways after the scan. She back home and Max back to work. She'd watched him leave, striding out towards the bike lockers without looking back.

Taking the scan photo out of her bag, she looked at it, a smile spreading across her face. She traced the outline of the babies' heads with her finger. She was going to have to do this alone. It was scary and exhilarating at the same time.

Now there were two babies, and only one of her. How was she ever going to manage all by herself?

She knew Max well enough to know that whether he wanted this or not he'd still feel responsible. And he'd want to do the right thing. What he thought the right thing was, she didn't know. But it clearly wasn't staying in London. Whatever it was that they'd had together had gone. It had been nothing more than a summer fling.

Had she repeated what had happened with Emilio? Stupidly allowed herself to fall for empty compliments and be swept away by the charms of a charismatic, emotionally disconnected man?

It was too easy to think that. Thinking that would reduce Max to the same level as Emilio, and that just wasn't the case. Max had meant what he'd said. He'd single-handedly slayed the dragon that her mother's words had created and that had been with her ever since she'd said them. Max had taught her to truly embrace her curves, to genuinely appreciate herself for who she was—to free herself from the chains of her past and believe in her own worth.

And she loved him for that. She always would. Even though he hadn't loved her enough to want to stay and make it work between them.

Placing the photo on the coffee table, she sat down on the sofa. He hadn't left yet but she missed him already. Glancing around the room, she took in the familiar objects…shelves full of books, knick-knacks from her travels. Candles, cushions, throws and rugs scattered around. It was her sanctuary—a cornucopia of the things she treasured. And it had felt complete with Max there. As if he'd been the final addition it had needed…the final treasure.

Before he'd arrived at St Martin's she'd expected an arrogant, egotistical surgeon—and she'd thought she'd witnessed that on day one, when they'd met. But little by little she'd begun to see chinks in his armour…clues to the man underneath the cool titanium plating he seemed to wear, and to the deeply caring nature that he chose to hide.

And the reason why he hid behind the impenetrable wall he'd built around himself was clear—he'd learnt to close his emotions down because the people he'd loved most in the world had closed down on him just when he'd needed them most. He could easily have given up—flunked school, never done anything with his life—and who could have blamed him? But he hadn't done that. He'd chosen a much more difficult path to walk. He'd tried to create something good out of something terrible.

Training to become a cardiac surgeon was tough, but he'd done it—even without his parents to support him. And now he'd come through again, with the screening programme. Max Templeton had been through hell and had responded by being more successful than most people ever got to be. And even though he still wore his armour, there were small fissures that, if she looked hard enough, she could peer through. And what she'd seen had made her want him even more.

But he was leaving. And although knowing that had been her safety net when she'd allowed him into her life, what she'd seen since then had made her realise that, actually, she really wanted more time with him.

In challenging, life-threatening situations on the ITU, when he showed what some might see as over-confidence, snappiness and even egotism on his part, she saw what was really going on in his head... He was simply concentrating. Giving everything he had to save his patient and remembering what happened with William.

But Max had made it clear from the start that he was going to a new life in California. He'd set out the boundaries of their... *What had it been?* An affair? A liaison? A summer fling? And finding out she was having his babies hadn't changed that. She wasn't enough for him. But that wasn't news... she'd known that from the start.

There was a knock at the door.

CHAPTER SEVENTEEN

'MAX!'

'Can I come in?'

She opened the door wider and stood back. 'Of course.'

He kicked off his shoes and walked through to the lounge.

'Would you like a coffee?'

'I'm not staying.'

She lowered her eyes and his stomach clenched—it was just a tiny hint that once more he'd hurt her.

'Okay. Well, have a seat anyway.'

He sank into the sofa and she sat down beside him with her feet curled up beside her in the way she always did. Candles flickered in their little glass jars. Everything was as it had always been. Like a home. Only one thing was different.

There was a new photo.

Black and white.

On the coffee table.

Propped up in front of a pile of books.

Their twin babies.

Please be okay. Don't let me have cursed you.

'You okay, Max?'

'We should talk.'

'Okay…'

But his carefully rehearsed words had disappeared without trace—had abandoned him just when he needed them.

The decision he'd come to had been easy to make. He was going to be a father and he had to face that…even though everything about it terrified him. What good could he be to any of them? He'd already hurt Lois and given the babies a heart condition that meant they'd need surgery even before they were born and would need monitoring and treatment for their entire lives.

He'd done enough damage, and now he needed to do whatever it took to put that right.

'It's my last shift tomorrow,' he said.

'Yes, I know. I'm not on shift so I won't see you.'

'I just wanted to see you before I go…to let you know what I propose.'

'Right.'

Her eyes searched his. She was waiting for him to say more.

'I'll come back for the twenty-week scan, so that I can supervise the screening and the surgery—even though I can't actually do it myself.'

'You don't need to do that.'

'I'm not going to shirk my responsibility, Lois. You know the risks you're facing, and I'm the one who's best placed to oversee things.'

'You're still talking as though the twins have the condition. They might be fine.'

'I'm glad you think that. But, as I've told you, the statistics show—'

She stood up, her eyes flashing with anger. 'Stop! I refuse to worry about something that may never happen. You don't need to come back to London once you've left. I don't need you to. It's more than obvious that you don't want anything to do with me or the twins…so just go. I absolutely refuse to allow you to come back here out of some sort of misplaced sense of responsibility. You feel guilty, Max, and that's crazy—this took both of us. I don't want you to come back just because you feel guilty.'

'You have no idea what I feel.'

His voice was low. Guilt was only one of the myriad emotions that had been keeping him awake at night. Try adding remorse, shame, anger and fear—that would be a little nearer to the mark.

Her eyes glittered. 'So tell me,' she said. 'I'd love to know, Max… You're such a closed book, I really have no idea. Why is the fact that we're going to be parents so bad? Why do you have to be so damn negative about this?'

'William died because of me.'

Why was he telling her this?

This wasn't part of the speech he'd so carefully prepared.

She took a step back, away from him. 'What do you mean? Of course he didn't. He had a heart condition.'

'He collapsed in front of me…and I didn't do anything.'

'You were twelve years old, Max. You couldn't have done anything.'

'I could have called an ambulance…started CPR. But I didn't. I froze…did nothing.' He plunged the knife deeper into his heart. 'I did nothing to help my brother.'

Lois stared at him as though he'd confessed to murder. He might as well have done.

And then her face and her voice softened. 'You were a child, Max. It wasn't your fault.'

He rubbed the back of his neck. 'I didn't save him.'

And he couldn't look at her. Because he could hear pity in her voice and he didn't want to see it in her face. He didn't deserve it…didn't want it. He focussed on the candle on the table, which flickered its orange glow onto the photo of the twins.

'Would you expect a twelve-year-old today to save someone if they had a cardiac arrest?'

Of course he wouldn't.

He shook his head. 'That's not the point.'

'But it is, Max. It's exactly the point.'

Her voice was soft, full of concern, empathy and understanding. But he didn't want any of those things. He deserved to pay for his mistake.

'It's a completely unrealistic and totally unfair expectation that you've put on your twelve-year-old self.'

William would be alive today if he'd done the right thing—done something—protected him. He didn't deserve forgiveness. He'd pay for his failings that day for the rest of his life. And rightly so.

'You don't need to spend the rest of your life trying to put right what happened, Max. You were a young child. You're entirely blameless.'

The orange flame from the candle flickered more strongly, as though a breath of air had passed over it.

No one had ever said that to him before. At the time, everyone had been so wrapped up in the horror of what had happened no one had stopped to wonder if he felt guilt as much as he felt grief. Until now. Until Lois. But still he couldn't look at her.

'This is why you've reacted to the pregnancy like this, isn't it? Max, when William collapsed you couldn't possibly have known what had happened or what to do. You didn't do anything wrong or bad. You found yourself, through no fault of your own, in a situation which most adults and even many medical professionals would find extremely difficult. You didn't do anything wrong. You're a good person.'

His throat constricted and his mother's scornful face and disparaging words came back to him.

Anger welled up inside him and he couldn't hide it when he spoke. 'I'm *not* a good person, Lois. William was my twin. I should have been there for him and I wasn't. I ruined everything.'

'No, you didn't. It was a tragedy, but it wasn't of your making.'

He laughed…a harsh, sneering laugh. 'Try telling my mother that.'

'She doesn't blame you.'

And then he saw her expression change from one that showed she was sure about the truth of her words into one of confusion and then horror as she looked into his eyes.

'Does she?'

Everything had been padlocked securely away

in a vault in his head for over two decades. All the grief, the pain, the guilt. Now suddenly the padlock had snapped open, and the demons inside the vault streamed out as his mother's words ricocheted in his mind and fired like bullets from his mouth…

'"Why didn't you do something, Max? What were you thinking…? Nothing? You've destroyed us. Your father died of a broken heart because of you. Don't ever have children of your own and destroy another family. You have to make sure this gene dies out with you."'

His voice cracked on the final words and he glanced at Lois.

'Don't feel sorry for me, Lois. I hear what you're saying, but she's right. I vowed then that I'd make damn sure I never did this to another family…and now that's exactly what's happened. So how the hell can I be happy about it?'

She didn't need to speak. Her face told him what she was thinking. She was horrified. And so she should be. But better she knew what he was—knew that there was something so inherently wrong with him that even his own mother hated him. He dropped his gaze. He'd seen all he needed to.

'Max.'

Her voice was soft, gentle, but his fists clenched in response. He didn't want her pity.

'She's wrong.'

She took a step towards him, placed her hands on top of his fists and he looked at them. His knuckles were white.

'Look at me.'

But he could only gaze ahead, over her shoulder, at the candle in the little votive jar, its flame dancing happily as if nothing had happened…as if he hadn't just fired decades worth of hurt at her and finally ended everything they'd had. They'd had a summer of bliss together and he'd fired a missile at it.

Lois lifted his chin, forcing him to look at her. There was no pity in her eyes. Just truth, honesty and genuineness. And the tension that had clenched every part of him began to release its grip and melt away.

'William will always be with you, but you have to let go of the guilt.'

He shook his head. 'It'll never leave me. Maybe you're right, and my mother shouldn't really blame me… I don't know. But she's right that it is my responsibility to make sure I don't curse another child with the gene that could kill them and destroy those they leave behind.'

'William wouldn't want you to live with this burden on your shoulders.'

'It's been there for so long now that it's just part of who I am.'

'You can change. Let me help you to do that. Can I hold you?'

She looked uncertain, and he wondered if she realised just how she'd challenged him. He wanted nothing more than to be held by her. He wanted to be able to allow her to soothe his twelve-year-old self, who'd never been soothed by anyone. She got him. She understood. And he was grateful to her. In love with her. But he wasn't ready to forgive himself. In fact, he was even less likely to forgive himself now. Because now he was responsible for wrecking even more lives.

'I should get back.'

'To work? It's eight p.m.'

'I need to check on a patient with sepsis.'

He knew she wouldn't be able to argue with that. Even if she wanted him to stay, she'd have to let him go for a patient.

'Oh, okay. Will you come back after?'

'No.'

She nodded and took a step back. 'When is your flight?'

'Thursday.'

Two days. One more shift.

'Okay.'

He took her in for what might well be the last time as his heart broke in two…as he clenched his fists against speaking those three words… The three words that he'd both wanted and not wanted to say all summer. Even if he couldn't love her in the way she deserved, he should tell her he had done, in his own way, this summer. He'd fallen in love for the first and last time…with her. She should know that.

He got up from the sofa—the sofa big enough to fit a family of four.

Tell her.

But his mouth was dry. He walked out through

the kitchen, clenching his fists harder, his nails digging into his palms.

Last chance, Templeton. Now or never.

He reached the hall and slipped his shoes on.

She was standing behind him. He wanted to hold her.

But he'd done enough damage.

She deserved to know that she'd been more than a summer romance. She was having his babies.

'I did love you, Lois.'

And before he could register her reaction, he opened the door and walked out into the street... out of her life.

CHAPTER EIGHTEEN

THE NURSES' STATION was decked out in good luck balloons and there was a huge cake in the office with a golden film award on the top, and lettering which said *Good Luck in Hollywood!*

The staff had certainly pulled out all the stops, but the only genuine smile Max had managed all morning had been when he'd reviewed Harry Weston and seen that his patient had turned the corner after his sepsis diagnosis. It looked as though he was going to make a full recovery.

He'd smiled plenty, of course—how could he not when the staff had made such an effort for his send-off? But the smiles hadn't been because he was excited and looking forward to leaving London and starting his new life in California.

Today was supposed to feel good.

Tomorrow, when he boarded the plane, was meant to be the happiest day of his life so far.

But today didn't feel good.

And tomorrow wasn't going to be the happiest of his life.

Why?

Why, when this was what he'd worked his whole life for, dreamt about, wished would happen sooner?

He looked up at the bouquets of balloons bobbing on their ribbons and smiled at Daisy as she walked past the nurses' station.

Because he'd made the biggest mistake of his

life…and there was a pretty high benchmark already.

What have you done, Max? You've walked away from the only woman you've ever loved.

Idiot.

The story of his life.

'You coming to cut the cake, chief?' Jay was beaming at him. 'And I think they're expecting a little farewell speech.'

'I'm just checking some results.'

'Your transplant chap?' Jay sat down beside him at the desk as he scrolled through his patient's latest bloods.

'Yeah, white cell count is much better. Looks like he'll be okay.'

'Excellent,' said Jay. 'Come on, then. Let's go and get your swansong done whilst we've got both the early and the late shift here together.'

'I'll pop in in a bit,' he replied, still scrolling.

'Not putting it off, are you?' asked Jay. 'Are you having second thoughts about leaving us? Because if you are, you know there'll always be a place for you here.'

'Thanks, Jay; that's kind.'

'It's not kind,' the older surgeon replied. 'You're an excellent surgeon, Max—any hospital would welcome you with open arms. I just hope that California appreciates you. I know working over there has been your goal for a long time, and even though it'll be very different, and will take some getting used to, there comes a time in life when you have to do what's right for you—make that leap of faith, take a risk and do what will make you happy.'

Max looked up from the screen. Being with Lois made him happy. Looking into her eyes, holding her, having fun with her. This summer had been the happiest time in his life since…

'So, if you've thought it all through, and you're doing what's right for you,' continued Jay, 'then you have to go in search of what will make you happy.'

Lois made him happy.

So why was he about to throw all that away? Why couldn't he be happy about this pregnancy as Lois was?

Why was that so hard?

Suddenly everything seemed clear. How had he not seen it before? Lois was where his happiness lay. It wasn't in California.

What had he done?

Yes, he was terrified that the babies might have the same heart condition William had had. Yes, he was devastated that he was the cause of all this worrying and waiting, and the tests and possible treatment for Lois and the twins. And no, maybe he wasn't good enough for her—maybe he wasn't capable of bringing her the happiness she deserved. But everything was a risk. Life was a risk. And sometimes you had to take a risk to grow, to learn, to achieve something worth having.

And Lois was worth taking a risk for. She was worth risking everything for.

It might be way too late, but suddenly he knew what he needed to do.

He logged out of the computer and stood up. 'I need you to cover for me.'

'What? There's a party waiting for you.'

'I'll come back later,' said Max, sliding his stethoscope from around his neck and pushing it into his pocket. 'I need to do something first. Cover for me, Jay…please?'

'Of course,' said Jay. 'I'm only catching up on paperwork this afternoon, anyway, so take as long as you need.'

'You're a star,' replied Max, clapping him on the shoulder as he handed his bleep over to him.

His happiness lay with Lois…and the babies. Yes, there were risks involved, but if taking them gave him even half a chance at spending the rest of his life with Lois they were worth taking.

All he had to do now was tell her, hope she'd forgive him, and hope that she'd be prepared to take a risk on him too.

CHAPTER NINETEEN

LOIS LAY ON her mat amongst twenty other mums-to-be, who were at various stages in their pregnancies, listening to the yoga teacher's soothing but instructive voice telling them the importance of box breathing.

'In for four…hold for four…'

Lois held her breath, and had counted to seven before she opened her eyes to check if the suddenly silent yoga instructor was still there.

She was, but she was staring towards the door at the back of the room and blinking as though she couldn't understand what she was seeing.

Lois turned her head as everyone else did.

And gasped.

At the same moment everyone else did.

Max.

He stood there in the doorway.

Large as life and as devastatingly handsome as ever.

What was he doing here?

And how had he known she was here? The only person she'd told was Natalie. She'd confided everything to her friend yesterday, telling her not to say anything to anyone.

Ever since the first night they'd slept together she and Max had made sure that no one knew of their affair. She hadn't wanted to be in the papers, labelled as the latest notch on his bedpost, and Max had wanted to make sure that any publicity was focussed only on the screening programme rather than his personal life.

'Can I help you?' The yoga teacher had flushed a deep pink. 'Are you looking for someone?'

'I'm looking for Lois.'

There were more gasps. Deep blue laser-like eyes looked at her, and those pesky butterflies flew into action in her stomach.

Max didn't move.

'I've come to tell her that I love her. And that I'm sorry for being so stupid. And that, if she'll have me after everything, I want to stay here to be with her and the twins. Not because of some inbuilt sense of duty…but because I want to. More than anything.'

Lois sensed without seeing them that all eyes were suddenly focussed on her. He loved her. He'd said the same when he'd come to her flat after the scan. But he'd said it so quickly and then he'd left— and he'd said it in the past tense. But this was now. He was saying it now. He wanted her and he wanted the babies.

She rose to her feet.

The room was silent.

Max stood watching her, his eyes never leaving hers as she walked towards him.

She hadn't been just a summer romance.

He hadn't been rejecting her.

He'd been scared because he'd hurt her and he'd just needed more time to realise what he wanted.

To make his choice.

And he'd chosen her.

She picked up her pace and walked towards him, almost running the last few yards as he opened his arms and she flew into them. There were cheers, whistles and clapping and his arms closed in around her, pulling her in towards him.

'I think we just went public, Max.'

'I think it's about time we did. There's a leaving party going on at the unit right now. If you're sure about this, we could go there…tell everyone the good news.'

'Good news?'

'May I?' He held his hand over her belly.

She smiled, grasping his hand and guiding it, her smile widening as he touched her and looked at her, admiration in his eyes.

'Yes, good news, Lois. The best news. I've loved you for a longer time than I realised and I already love these two. What more could I ever have asked for?'

'I love you too, Max.' She turned back to the class. 'I may just duck out a little early, if that's okay? See you all next week?'

There was a chorus of 'Bye!' and 'See you next week!' And Max took her by the hand, holding the door open for her and letting it close quietly behind them.

'How did you find me?' she asked.

'Long story.' He grimaced. 'I tried the flat, but of course you weren't there. I called you, but there was no answer. So I rang Toby and asked for Natalie's number, spoke to her and she told me. Don't blame her—I was very insistent.'

Lois laughed. 'I won't blame her. Can we talk before we go into work?'

'Of course; let's sit here.'

There was a shady bench under a tree whose leaves were just showing the first signs of autumn, glowing orange in the early-afternoon sunlight.

'So what changed your mind?' asked Lois, sitting down and placing her gym bag on the seat beside her.

'It wasn't sudden, if I really think about it. It had been happening slowly…ever since I met you. The thought of California and the new job lost its sparkle…bit by bit. The more I got to know you, the less I wanted to leave.'

'But you seemed so determined to go…even yesterday.'

'I couldn't bear it that I'd hurt you.'

'You didn't.'

'I also couldn't bear it that I might never see you again. So I had a dilemma.'

'In what way?'

'I could run away, so that I didn't have to see what I was putting you through. Or I could spend the rest of my life regretting that and wondering if we could have been happy together.'

'You're not putting me through anything I don't want to go through, Max. I'm *glad* we met. I'm *glad* we had an amazing summer together.' She placed her hand over her belly. 'And I'm glad we're going to be parents to these two.'

'And are you glad I came to find you and made you the centre of attention just then? Or, since the show, have you realised that you *should* be the centre of attention? That you deserve to be?'

A woman walked past with her dog and did a double-take when she saw Max.

'I guess I'll have to get used to a bit of attention if I'm with you.'

'There are a few other risks in being with me.' He placed his hands over hers on her lap and looked deeply into her eyes. 'I can't offer any guarantee of a roses-round-the-door future.'

'Well, that makes us a good match…because neither can I. But what we *can* guarantee each other right now is that we love each other—and that's a pretty good starting point, if you ask me.'

CHAPTER TWENTY

LOIS TRIED DESPERATELY to slow her heart rate as the ultrasound probe made contact with her ever-growing belly. Max squeezed her hand and gave her a reassuring smile. But she knew that he was more nervous than she was. He'd tried to hide his fears over the two months they'd needed to wait to have the screening scan, but she knew he felt responsible for their shared nervousness.

Increasingly, over the last couple of weeks as the appointment had approached, he'd not slept well, and she'd awoken a few times at night and found him pacing around downstairs, wide awake. He'd tried to tell her that he was concerned about a patient, and she'd allowed him to think that she believed him. But, although he cared deeply about his patients, she knew what the real cause of his sleeplessness was. He was worried about the twins… and about her.

If either or both of the twins had the heart condition, she knew how he'd react. He'd be devastated. But she'd be there for him and they'd all get through it…whatever happened.

Jay Vallini stood to one side of the cardiac radiologist, watching the screen intently. The older consultant had given strict instructions. Today, Max was not a cardiac surgeon. Today he was a father, and he was there to support Lois. So Max had done

as he'd been told and was now holding her hand
rather than making a diagnosis.

Jay had been right when he'd assured Max that
if he wanted to stay on as a consultant at St Martin's he'd be welcomed with open arms. Max had
managed to get out of his contract in LA, and had
signed a full-time contract at the hospital. And he
really had been warmly welcomed as a permanent
member of staff.

Their relationship had been warmly welcomed
too. One or two of the staff had said they'd sensed
there was something between them. And Tom had
hugged her and said he wished he'd put money on
it because he'd 'just known'.

In a few moments they'd have the answer to the
question that had so nearly been the cause of their
break-up. Max's realisation that his love for her far
outweighed his fears and his guilt over what might
or might not happen with the twins' health, and the
fact that he was willing to risk telling her he loved
her, was what had saved them.

The pressure of Max's grip on her hand in-
creased. She looked at him and he managed a
smile…managed not to divert his gaze from her and
go into doctor mode and scrutinise the screen. He
was trusting the two consultants who were doing
that for them. And he was being there for her.

She steadied her breathing.

'Would you like to hear twin number one's heartbeat?' said Jay.

'Please,' replied Max, still looking at her. His jaw

was tight, but somehow he was managing a small smile…for her.

And there it was. The first heartbeat…fast but regular.

'Twin number one is fine,' said the radiologist, still staring at the screen.

De-dum…de-dum…de-dum.

He moved the probe to twin number two and the sound faded before being picked up again.

Lois held her breath and closed her eyes.

Please be okay.

There was a long minute while the radiologist took measurements.

De-dum…de-dum…de-dum.

'And so is twin two. They're both fine—no heart issues whatsoever.'

Lois opened her eyes. Max had let his head fall back, and his eyes were closed. But when he opened them and looked at her his eyes shone with a fusion of relief, gratitude and the release of weeks of bottled-up dread and fear.

She smiled at him. He cared so much…about all of them. 'They're okay, Max.'

He nodded slowly.

'We're going to nip out and give you two a few moments,' said Jay.

'Thank you…both of you,' said Max, his voice thick with emotion.

'So your mother was wrong, Max. You didn't need to vow never to have children. You have two healthy children right here.'

'And *your* mother was wrong, too,' he replied,

smiling at her. 'You're the most perfect, beautiful, gorgeous woman in the world, and you're going to be an amazing mum…and wife…if you'll have me.'

'Wife?'

'I know this isn't the most romantic proposal in the world…maybe I'll have to whisk you away somewhere more special and repeat it another time to make up for it… But I love you, Lois Newington. Completely. I want to build a life with you and raise our family together. Will you marry me?'

He hadn't let go of her hand even for one second throughout the whole procedure and he still held it now. And she knew that she could trust him never to let it go…*ever*.

'You don't need to whisk me away somewhere more special, Max. Where could be more perfect than the place where we found out we're having two healthy twins? Yes, of course I'll marry you.'

And as she lifted her arms, and he bent towards her to take her into his own, she took a long, deep, contented breath, drawing him in, knowing that she'd be able to do that for the rest of her life.

EPILOGUE

EVEN AT ONLY eighteen months old, the twins were proper water babies. Lois laughed as she placed a tray of drinks down on the table by the outdoor pool, watching them splashing around with Max in the sunshine.

Moving to the countryside had been a joint decision. Max continued to practise in London, but they had a huge house and an enormous garden for their growing family to live in. And with baby number three on the way, it was proving to be a good move.

'Come on in,' called Max, dodging as the twins, with delighted squeals, threw the beach ball at him in turn.

Lois slipped the sarong from her shoulders and kicked off her flip-flops. The blue swimsuit didn't hold her in all the right places, because she was four months pregnant and no swimsuit would. But it didn't matter. Max loved her just as she was. And she knew that because he told her every day. And if he didn't tell her, he showed it. In all sorts of ways.

'Mummy, throw ball!' called William, batting the brightly coloured ball with his chubby little hand.

Max waded over to her where she sat on the edge of the pool, dangling her legs in the water. 'Coming in?'

'I might just sit here and watch.'

She loved watching Max with the children. It only strengthened the knowledge that she'd done the right thing that day when he'd come back to tell her he loved her…loved her so much that he'd been prepared to hurt himself to protect her.

'Mummy, in pool,' said Isabel, kicking her legs ferociously to propel her and her inflatable ring towards her.

'Mummy's coming in.' Max took her by the waist, lifting her into the water as she laughed. 'Let's get her all wet, kids.'

William and Isabel squealed with laughter as they splashed her, laughing even more as Lois made unsuccessful attempts to shield herself from the watery onslaught.

'My hair!'

But Lois knew there was no point in trying to object. It would just make all three of them scream even louder with laughter and try even harder to soak her completely. But she didn't mind. Max had turned her world upside down and given her a life she'd never even dared to dream of…a family she couldn't have loved more if she tried.

'Your hair is perfect, Mrs Templeton.' Holding her to him, he kissed her. 'And even if it wasn't, I'd still fancy you like crazy.'

Somehow the twins had managed to manoeuvre themselves in their inflatable rings so that there was one on either side of them, trying to elbow their way between them.

'Mummy! Dada!'

They both laughed.

'Well, just remember where fancying me like

crazy got you last time,' said Lois, glancing down at William and Isabel and grinning.

'It got me a life more perfect than I could ever have imagined and I wouldn't change a thing. I love you, Mrs Templeton.'

'Love you t—'

But Lois couldn't finish her sentence, because suddenly the twins, moving as one, as though having planned it with some sort of twin telepathy, splashed her with such a volume of water that her words were swallowed with a mouthful of pool water.

Squeals of delight told her that her shocked expression must be hilarious, and joining in with their laughter was impossible not to do.

'Oops…' said Max, grinning, his dark hair even darker for being wet and his blue eyes sparkling with joy.

She scooped up a handful of water and it flew in a glittering arc, cascading over all four of them in sparkling, sunlit droplets. Over her family. Her whole world.

* * * * *

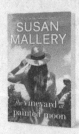